PHANTASTES
A FAERIE ROMANCE FOR MEN AND WOMEN

By George Macdonald

"In good sooth, my masters, this is no door.

Yet is it a little window, that looketh upon a great world."

CONTENTS

PREFACE

For offering this new edition of my father's Phantastes, my reasons are three. The first is to rescue the work from an edition illustrated without the author's sanction, and so unsuitably that all lovers of the book must have experienced some real grief in turning its pages. With the copyright I secured also the whole of that edition and turned it into pulp.

My second reason is to pay a small tribute to my father by way of personal gratitude for this, his first prose work, which was published nearly fifty years ago. Though unknown to many lovers of his greater writings, none of these has exceeded it in imaginative insight and power of expression. To me it rings with the dominant chord of his life's purpose and work.

My third reason is that wider knowledge and love of the book should be made possible. To this end I have been most happy in the help of my father's old friend, who has illustrated the book. I know of no other living artist who is capable of portraying the spirit of Phantastes; and every reader of this edition will, I believe, feel that the illustrations are a part of the romance, and will gain through them some perception of the brotherhood between George MacDonald and Arthur Hughes.
GREVILLE MACDONALD.
September 1905.

PHANTASTES A FAERIE ROMANCE
"Phantastes from 'their fount' all shapes deriving,
In new habiliments can quickly dight."
FLETCHER'S Purple Island

Es lassen sich Erzählungen ohne Zusammenhang, jedoch mit Association, wie Träume, denken; Gedichte, die bloss wohlklingend und voll schöner Worte sind, aber auch ohne allen Sinn und Zusammenhang, höchstens einzelne Strophen verständlich, wie Bruchstücke aus den verschiedenartigsten Dingen. Diese wahre Poesie kann höchstens einen allegorischen Sinn in Grossen, und eine indirecte Wirkung, wie Musik, haben. Darum ist die Natur so rein poetisch, wie die Stube eines Zauberers, eines Physikers, eine Kinderstube, eine Polter- und Vorrathskammer.

Ein Märchen ist wie ein Traumbild ohne Zusammenhang. Ein Ensemble wunderbarer Dinge und Begebenheiten, z. B. eine musikalische Phantasie, die harmonischen Folgen einer Aeolsharfe, die Natur selbst...

In einem echten Märchen muss alles wunderbar, geheimnissvoll und zusammenhängend sein; alles belebt, jeder auf eine andere Art. Die ganze Natur muss wunderlich mit der ganzen Geisterwelt gemischt sein; hier tritt die Zeit der Anarchie, der Gesetzlosigkeit, Freiheit, der Naturstand der Natur, die Zeit von der Welt ein . . . Die Welt des Märchens ist die, der Welt der Wahrheit durchaus entgegengesetzte, und eben darum ihr so durchaus ähnlich, wie das Chaos der vollendeten Schöpfung ähnlich ist.--NOVALIS.

CHAPTER I

"A spirit . . .

. . . . . .
The undulating and silent well,
And rippling rivulet, and evening gloom,
Now deepening the dark shades, for speech assuming,
Held commune with him; as if he and it
Were all that was."
SHELLEY'S Alastor.

I awoke one morning with the usual perplexity of mind which accompanies the return of consciousness. As I lay and looked through the eastern window of my room, a faint streak of peach-colour, dividing a cloud that just rose above the low swell of the horizon, announced the approach of the sun. As my thoughts, which a deep and apparently dreamless sleep had dissolved, began again to assume crystalline forms, the strange events of the foregoing night presented themselves anew to my wondering consciousness. The day before had been my one-and-twentieth birthday. Among other ceremonies investing me with my legal rights, the keys of an old secretary, in which my father had kept his private papers, had been delivered up to me. As soon as I was left alone, I ordered lights in the chamber where the secretary stood, the first lights that had been there for many a year; for, since my father's death, the room had been left undisturbed. But, as if the darkness had been too long an inmate to be easily expelled, and had dyed with blackness the walls to which, bat-like, it had clung, these tapers served but ill to light up the gloomy hangings, and seemed to throw yet darker shadows into the hollows of the deep-wrought cornice. All the further portions of the room lay shrouded in a mystery whose deepest folds were gathered around the dark oak cabinet which I now approached with a strange mingling of reverence and curiosity. Perhaps, like a geologist, I was about to turn up to the light some of the buried strata of the human world, with its fossil remains charred by passion and petrified by tears. Perhaps I was to learn how my father, whose personal history was unknown to me, had woven his web of story; how he had found the world, and how the world had left him. Perhaps I was to find only the records of lands and moneys, how gotten and how secured; coming down from strange men, and through troublous times, to me, who knew little or nothing of them all. To solve my speculations, and to dispel the awe which was fast gathering around me as if the dead were drawing near, I approached the secretary; and having found the key that fitted the upper portion, I opened it with some difficulty, drew near it a heavy high-backed chair, and sat down before a multitude of little drawers and slides and pigeon-holes. But the door of a little cupboard in the centre especially attracted my interest, as if there lay the secret of this long-hidden world. Its key I found.

One of the rusty hinges cracked and broke as I opened the door: it revealed a number of small pigeon-holes. These, however, being but shallow compared with the depth of those around the little cupboard, the outer ones reaching to the back of the desk, I concluded that there must be some accessible space behind; and found, indeed, that they were formed in a separate framework, which admitted of the whole being pulled out in one piece. Behind, I found a sort of flexible portcullis of small bars of wood laid close together horizontally. After long search, and trying many ways to move it, I discovered at last a scarcely projecting point of steel on one side. I pressed this repeatedly and hard with the point of an old tool that was lying near, till at length it yielded inwards; and the little slide, flying up suddenly, disclosed a chamber— empty, except that in one corner lay a little heap of withered rose-leaves, whose long-lived scent had long since departed; and, in another, a small packet of papers, tied with a bit of ribbon, whose colour had gone with the rose-scent. Almost fearing to touch them, they witnessed so mutely to the law of oblivion, I leaned back in my chair, and regarded them for a moment; when suddenly there stood on the threshold of the little chamber, as though she had just emerged from its depth, a tiny woman-form, as perfect in shape as if she had been a small Greek statuette roused to life and motion. Her dress was of a kind that could never grow old-fashioned, because it was simply natural: a robe plaited in a band around the neck, and confined by a belt about the waist, descended to her feet. It was only afterwards, however, that I took notice of her dress, although my surprise was by no means of so overpowering a degree as such an apparition might naturally be expected to excite. Seeing, however, as I suppose, some astonishment in my countenance, she came forward within a yard of me, and said, in a voice that strangely recalled a sensation of twilight, and reedy river banks, and a low wind, even in this deathly room:—

"Anodos, you never saw such a little creature before, did you?"

"No," said I; "and indeed I hardly believe I do now."

"Ah! that is always the way with you men; you believe nothing the first time; and it is foolish enough to let mere repetition convince you of what you consider in itself unbelievable. I am not going to argue with you, however, but to grant you a wish."

Here I could not help interrupting her with the foolish speech, of which, however, I had no cause to repent—

"How can such a very little creature as you grant or refuse anything?"

"Is that all the philosophy you have gained in one-and-twenty years?" said she. "Form is much, but size is nothing. It is a mere matter of relation. I suppose your six-foot lordship does not feel altogether insignificant, though to others you do look small beside your old Uncle Ralph, who rises above you a great half-foot at least. But size is of so little consequence with old me, that I may as well accommodate myself to your foolish prejudices."

So saying, she leapt from the desk upon the floor, where she stood a tall, gracious lady, with pale face and large blue eyes. Her dark hair flowed behind, wavy but uncurled, down to her waist, and against it her form stood clear in its robe of white.

"Now," said she, "you will believe me."

Overcome with the presence of a beauty which I could now perceive, and drawn towards her by an attraction irresistible as incomprehensible, I suppose I stretched out my arms towards her, for she drew back a step or two, and said—

"Foolish boy, if you could touch me, I should hurt you. Besides, I was two hundred and thirty-seven years old, last Midsummer eve; and a man must not fall in love with his grandmother, you know."

"But you are not my grandmother," said I.

"How do you know that?" she retorted. "I dare say you know something of your great-grandfathers a good deal further back than that; but you know very little about your great-grandmothers on either side. Now, to the point. Your little sister was reading a fairy-tale to you last night."

"She was."

"When she had finished, she said, as she closed the book, 'Is there a fairy-country, brother?' You replied with a sigh, 'I suppose there is, if one could find the way into it.'"

"I did; but I meant something quite different from what you seem to think."

"Never mind what I seem to think. You shall find the way into Fairy Land to-morrow. Now look in my eyes."

Eagerly I did so. They filled me with an unknown longing. I remembered somehow that my mother died when I was a baby. I looked deeper and deeper, till they spread around me like seas, and I sank in their waters. I forgot all the rest, till I found myself at the window, whose gloomy curtains were withdrawn, and where I stood gazing on a whole heaven of stars, small and sparkling in the moonlight. Below lay a sea, still as death and hoary in the moon, sweeping into bays and around capes and islands, away, away, I knew not whither. Alas! it was no sea, but a low bog burnished by the moon. "Surely there is such a sea somewhere!" said I to myself. A low sweet voice beside me replied—

"In Fairy Land, Anodos."

I turned, but saw no one. I closed the secretary, and went to my own room, and to bed.

All this I recalled as I lay with half-closed eyes. I was soon to find the truth of the lady's promise, that this day I should discover the road into Fairy Land.

CHAPTER II

"'Where is the stream?' cried he, with tears. 'Seest thou its not in blue waves above us?' He looked up, and lo! the blue stream was flowing gently over their heads."
—NOVALIS, Heinrich von Ofterdingen.

While these strange events were passing through my mind, I suddenly, as one awakes to the consciousness that the sea has been moaning by him for hours, or that the storm has been howling about his window all night, became aware of the sound of running water near me; and, looking out of bed, I saw that a large green marble basin, in which I was wont to wash, and which stood on a low pedestal of the same material in a corner of my room, was overflowing like a spring; and that a stream of clear water was running over the carpet, all the length of the room, finding its outlet I knew not where. And, stranger still, where this carpet, which I had myself designed to imitate a field of grass and daisies, bordered the course of the little stream, the grass-blades and daisies seemed to wave in a tiny breeze that followed the water's flow; while under the rivulet they bent and swayed with every motion of the changeful current, as if they were about to dissolve with it, and, forsaking their fixed form, become fluent as the waters.

My dressing-table was an old-fashioned piece of furniture of black oak, with drawers all down the front. These were elaborately carved in foliage, of which ivy formed the chief part. The nearer end of this table remained just as it had been, but on the further end a singular change had commenced. I happened to fix my eye on a little cluster of ivy-leaves. The first of these was evidently the work of the carver; the next looked curious; the third was unmistakable ivy; and just beyond it a tendril of clematis had twined itself about the gilt handle of one of the drawers. Hearing next a slight motion above me, I looked up, and saw that the branches and leaves designed upon the curtains of my bed were slightly in motion. Not knowing what change might follow next, I thought it high time to get up; and, springing from the bed, my bare feet alighted upon a cool green sward; and although I dressed in all haste, I found myself completing my toilet under the boughs of a great tree, whose top waved in the golden stream of the sunrise with many interchanging lights, and with shadows of leaf and branch gliding over leaf and branch, as the cool morning wind swung it to and fro, like a sinking sea-wave.

After washing as well as I could in the clear stream, I rose and looked around me. The tree under which I seemed to have lain all night was one of the advanced guard of a dense forest, towards which the rivulet ran. Faint traces of a footpath, much overgrown with grass and moss, and with here and there a pimpernel even, were discernible along the right bank. "This," thought I, "must surely be the path into Fairy Land, which the lady of last night promised I should so soon find." I crossed the rivulet, and accompanied it, keeping the footpath on its right bank, until it led me, as I expected, into the wood. Here I left it, without any good reason: and with a vague feeling that I ought to have followed its course, I took a more southerly direction.

CHAPTER III

"Man doth usurp all space,
Stares thee, in rock, bush, river, in
the face.
Never thine eyes behold a tree;
'Tis no sea thou seest in the sea,
'Tis but a disguised humanity.
To avoid thy fellow, vain thy plan;
All that interests a man, is man."
HENRY SUTTON.

The trees, which were far apart where I entered, giving free passage to the level rays of the sun, closed rapidly as I advanced, so that ere long their crowded stems barred the sunlight out, forming as it were a thick grating between me and the East. I seemed to be advancing towards a second midnight. In the midst of the intervening twilight, however, before I entered what appeared to be the darkest portion of the forest, I saw a country maiden coming towards me from its very depths. She did not seem to observe me, for she was apparently intent upon a bunch of wild flowers which she carried in her hand. I could hardly see her face; for, though she came direct towards me, she never looked up. But when we met, instead of passing, she turned and walked alongside of me for a few yards, still keeping her face downwards, and busied with her flowers. She spoke rapidly, however, all the time, in a low tone, as if talking to herself, but evidently addressing the purport of her words to me.

She seemed afraid of being observed by some lurking foe. "Trust the Oak," said she; "trust the Oak, and the Elm, and the great Beech. Take care of the Birch, for though she is honest, she is too young not to be changeable. But shun the Ash and the Alder; for the Ash is an ogre,—you will know him by his thick fingers; and the Alder will smother you with her web of hair, if you let her near you at night." All this was uttered without pause or alteration of tone. Then she turned suddenly and left me, walking still with the same unchanging gait. I could not conjecture what she meant, but satisfied myself with thinking that it would be time enough to find out her meaning when there was need to make use of her warning, and that the occasion would reveal the admonition. I concluded from the flowers that she carried, that the forest could not be everywhere so dense as it appeared from where I was now walking; and I was right in this conclusion. For soon I came to a more

8

open part, and by-and-by crossed a wide grassy glade, on which were several circles of brighter green. But even here I was struck with the utter stillness. No bird sang. No insect hummed. Not a living creature crossed my way. Yet somehow the whole environment seemed only asleep, and to wear even in sleep an air of expectation. The trees seemed all to have an expression of conscious mystery, as if they said to themselves, "we could, an' if we would." They had all a meaning look about them. Then I remembered that night is the fairies' day, and the moon their sun; and I thought—Everything sleeps and dreams now: when the night comes, it will be different. At the same time I, being a man and a child of the day, felt some anxiety as to how I should fare among the elves and other children of the night who wake when mortals dream, and find their common life in those wondrous hours that flow noiselessly over the moveless death-like forms of men and women and children, lying strewn and parted beneath the weight of the heavy waves of night, which flow on and beat them down, and hold them drowned and senseless, until the ebbtide comes, and the waves sink away, back into the ocean of the dark. But I took courage and went on. Soon, however, I became again anxious, though from another cause. I had eaten nothing that day, and for an hour past had been feeling the want of food. So I grew afraid lest I should find nothing to meet my human necessities in this strange place; but once more I comforted myself with hope and went on.

Before noon, I fancied I saw a thin blue smoke rising amongst the stems of larger trees in front of me; and soon I came to an open spot of ground in which stood a little cottage, so built that the stems of four great trees formed its corners, while their branches met and intertwined over its roof, heaping a great cloud of leaves over it, up towards the heavens. I wondered at finding a human dwelling in this neighbourhood; and yet it did not look altogether human, though sufficiently so to encourage me to expect to find some sort of food. Seeing no door, I went round to the other side, and there I found one, wide open. A woman sat beside it, preparing some vegetables for dinner. This was homely and comforting. As I came near, she looked up, and seeing me, showed no surprise, but bent her head again over her work, and said in a low tone:

"Did you see my daughter?"

"I believe I did," said I. "Can you give me something to eat, for I am very hungry?" "With pleasure," she replied, in the same tone; "but do not say anything more, till you come into the house, for the Ash is watching us."

Having said this, she rose and led the way into the cottage; which, I now saw, was built of the stems of small trees set closely together, and was

9

furnished with rough chairs and tables, from which even the bark had not been removed. As soon as she had shut the door and set a chair—

"You have fairy blood in you," said she, looking hard at me.

"How do you know that?"

"You could not have got so far into this wood if it were not so; and I am trying to find out some trace of it in your countenance. I think I see it."

"What do you see?"

"Oh, never mind: I may be mistaken in that."

"But how then do you come to live here?"

"Because I too have fairy blood in me."

Here I, in my turn, looked hard at her, and thought I could perceive, notwithstanding the coarseness of her features, and especially the heaviness of her eyebrows, a something unusual—I could hardly call it grace, and yet it was an expression that strangely contrasted with the form of her features. I noticed too that her hands were delicately formed, though brown with work and exposure.

"I should be ill," she continued, "if I did not live on the borders of the fairies' country, and now and then eat of their food. And I see by your eyes that you are not quite free of the same need; though, from your education and the activity of your mind, you have felt it less than I. You may be further removed too from the fairy race."

I remembered what the lady had said about my grandmothers.

Here she placed some bread and some milk before me, with a kindly apology for the homeliness of the fare, with which, however, I was in no humour to quarrel. I now thought it time to try to get some explanation of the strange words both of her daughter and herself.

"What did you mean by speaking so about the Ash?"

She rose and looked out of the little window. My eyes followed her; but as the window was too small to allow anything to be seen from where I was sitting, I rose and looked over her shoulder. I had just time to see, across the open space, on the edge of the denser forest, a single large ash-tree, whose foliage showed bluish, amidst the truer green of the other trees around it; when she pushed me back with an expression of impatience and terror, and then almost shut out the light from the window by setting up a large old book in it.

"In general," said she, recovering her composure, "there is no danger in the daytime, for then he is sound asleep; but there is something unusual going on in the woods; there must be some solemnity among the fairies to-night, for all the trees are restless, and although they cannot come awake, they see and hear in their sleep."

"But what danger is to be dreaded from him?"

Instead of answering the question, she went again to the window and looked out, saying she feared the fairies would be interrupted by foul weather, for a storm was brewing in the west.

"And the sooner it grows dark, the sooner the Ash will be awake," added she.

I asked her how she knew that there was any unusual excitement in the woods. She replied—

"Besides the look of the trees, the dog there is unhappy; and the eyes and ears of the white rabbit are redder than usual, and he frisks about as if he expected some fun. If the cat were at home, she would have her back up; for the young fairies pull the sparks out of her tail with bramble thorns, and she knows when they are coming. So do I, in another way."

At this instant, a grey cat rushed in like a demon, and disappeared in a hole in the wall.

"There, I told you!" said the woman.

"But what of the ash-tree?" said I, returning once more to the subject. Here, however, the young woman, whom I had met in the morning, entered. A smile passed between the mother and daughter; and then the latter began to help her mother in little household duties.

"I should like to stay here till the evening," I said; "and then go on my journey, if you will allow me."

"You are welcome to do as you please; only it might be better to stay all night, than risk the dangers of the wood then. Where are you going?"

"Nay, that I do not know," I replied, "but I wish to see all that is to be seen, and therefore I should like to start just at sundown." "You are a bold youth, if you have any idea of what you are daring; but a rash one, if you know nothing about it; and, excuse me, you do not seem very well informed about the country and its manners. However, no one comes here but for some reason, either known to himself or to those who have charge of him; so you shall do just as you wish."

Accordingly I sat down, and feeling rather tired, and disinclined for further talk, I asked leave to look at the old book which still screened the window. The woman brought it to me directly, but not before taking another look towards the forest, and then drawing a white blind over the window. I sat down opposite to it by the table, on which I laid the great old volume, and read. It contained many wondrous tales of Fairy Land, and olden times, and the Knights of King Arthur's table. I read on and on, till the shades of the afternoon began to deepen; for in the midst of the forest it gloomed earlier than in the open country. At length I came to this passage—

"Here it chanced, that upon their quest, Sir Galahad and Sir Percivale rencountered in the depths of a great forest. Now, Sir Galahad was dight all in harness of silver, clear and shining; the which is a delight to look

11

upon, but full hasty to tarnish, and withouten the labour of a ready squire, uneath to be kept fair and clean. And yet withouten squire or page, Sir Galahad's armour shone like the moon. And he rode a great white mare, whose bases and other housings were black, but all besprent with fair lilys of silver sheen. Whereas Sir Percivale bestrode a red horse, with a tawny mane and tail; whose trappings were all to-smirched with mud and mire; and his armour was wondrous rosty to behold, ne could he by any art furbish it again; so that as the sun in his going down shone twixt the bare trunks of the trees, full upon the knights twain, the one did seem all shining with light, and the other all to glow with ruddy fire. Now it came about in this wise. For Sir Percivale, after his escape from the demon lady, whenas the cross on the handle of his sword smote him to the heart, and he rove himself through the thigh, and escaped away, he came to a great wood; and, in nowise cured of his fault, yet bemoaning the same, the damosel of the alder tree encountered him, right fair to see; and with her fair words and false countenance she comforted him and beguiled him, until he followed her where she led him to a——"

Here a low hurried cry from my hostess caused me to look up from the book, and I read no more.

"Look there!" she said; "look at his fingers!"

Just as I had been reading in the book, the setting sun was shining through a cleft in the clouds piled up in the west; and a shadow as of a large distorted hand, with thick knobs and humps on the fingers, so that it was much wider across the fingers than across the undivided part of the hand, passed slowly over the little blind, and then as slowly returned in the opposite direction.

"He is almost awake, mother; and greedier than usual to-night."

"Hush, child; you need not make him more angry with us than he is; for you do not know how soon something may happen to oblige us to be in the forest after nightfall."

"But you are in the forest," said I; "how is it that you are safe here?"

"He dares not come nearer than he is now," she replied; "for any of those four oaks, at the corners of our cottage, would tear him to pieces; they are our friends. But he stands there and makes awful faces at us sometimes, and stretches out his long arms and fingers, and tries to kill us with fright; for, indeed, that is his favourite way of doing. Pray, keep out of his way to-night."

"Shall I be able to see these things?" said I.

"That I cannot tell yet, not knowing how much of the fairy nature there is in you. But we shall soon see whether you can discern the fairies in my little garden, and that will be some guide to us."

"Are the trees fairies too, as well as the flowers?" I asked.

12

"They are of the same race," she replied; "though those you call fairies in your country are chiefly the young children of the flower fairies. They are very fond of having fun with the thick people, as they call you; for, like most children, they like fun better than anything else."

"Why do you have flowers so near you then? Do they not annoy you?"

"Oh, no, they are very amusing, with their mimicries of grown people, and mock solemnities. Sometimes they will act a whole play through before my eyes, with perfect composure and assurance, for they are not afraid of me. Only, as soon as they have done, they burst into peals of tiny laughter, as if it was such a joke to have been serious over anything. These I speak of, however, are the fairies of the garden. They are more staid and educated than those of the fields and woods. Of course they have near relations amongst the wild flowers, but they patronise them, and treat them as country cousins, who know nothing of life, and very little of manners. Now and then, however, they are compelled to envy the grace and simplicity of the natural flowers."

"Do they live *in* the flowers?" I said.

"I cannot tell," she replied. "There is something in it I do not understand. Sometimes they disappear altogether, even from me, though I know they are near. They seem to die always with the flowers they resemble, and by whose names they are called; but whether they return to life with the fresh flowers, or, whether it be new flowers, new fairies, I cannot tell. They have as many sorts of dispositions as men and women, while their moods are yet more variable; twenty different expressions will cross their little faces in half a minute. I often amuse myself with watching them, but I have never been able to make personal acquaintance with any of them. If I speak to one, he or she looks up in my face, as if I were not worth heeding, gives a little laugh, and runs away." Here the woman started, as if suddenly recollecting herself, and said in a low voice to her daughter, "Make haste—go and watch him, and see in what direction he goes."

I may as well mention here, that the conclusion I arrived at from the observations I was afterwards able to make, was, that the flowers die because the fairies go away; not that the fairies disappear because the flowers die. The flowers seem a sort of houses for them, or outer bodies, which they can put on or off when they please. Just as you could form some idea of the nature of a man from the kind of house he built, if he followed his own taste, so you could, without seeing the fairies, tell what any one of them is like, by looking at the flower till you feel that you understand it. For just what the flower says to you, would the face and form of the fairy say; only so much more plainly as a face and human figure can express more than a flower. For the house or the clothes,

13

though like the inhabitant or the wearer, cannot be wrought into an equal power of utterance. Yet you would see a strange resemblance, almost oneness, between the flower and the fairy, which you could not describe, but which described itself to you. Whether all the flowers have fairies, I cannot determine, any more than I can be sure whether all men and women have souls.

The woman and I continued the conversation for a few minutes longer. I was much interested by the information she gave me, and astonished at the language in which she was able to convey it. It seemed that intercourse with the fairies was no bad education in itself. But now the daughter returned with the news, that the Ash had just gone away in a south-westerly direction; and, as my course seemed to lie eastward, she hoped I should be in no danger of meeting him if I departed at once. I looked out of the little window, and there stood the ash-tree, to my eyes the same as before; but I believed that they knew better than I did, and prepared to go. I pulled out my purse, but to my dismay there was nothing in it. The woman with a smile begged me not to trouble myself, for money was not of the slightest use there; and as I might meet with people in my journeys whom I could not recognise to be fairies, it was well I had no money to offer, for nothing offended them so much.

"They would think," she added, "that you were making game of them; and that is their peculiar privilege with regard to us." So we went together into the little garden which sloped down towards a lower part of the wood.

Here, to my great pleasure, all was life and bustle. There was still light enough from the day to see a little; and the pale half-moon, halfway to the zenith, was reviving every moment. The whole garden was like a carnival, with tiny, gaily decorated forms, in groups, assemblies, processions, pairs or trios, moving stately on, running about wildly, or sauntering hither or thither. From the cups or bells of tall flowers, as from balconies, some looked down on the masses below, now bursting with laughter, now grave as owls; but even in their deepest solemnity, seeming only to be waiting for the arrival of the next laugh. Some were launched on a little marshy stream at the bottom, in boats chosen from the heaps of last year's leaves that lay about, curled and withered. These soon sank with them; whereupon they swam ashore and got others. Those who took fresh rose-leaves for their boats floated the longest; but for these they had to fight; for the fairy of the rose-tree complained bitterly that they were stealing her clothes, and defended her property bravely.

"You can't wear half you've got," said some.

"Never you mind; I don't choose you to have them: they are my property."

"All for the good of the community!" said one, and ran off with a great hollow leaf. But the rose-fairy sprang after him (what a beauty she was! only too like a drawing-room young lady), knocked him heels-over-head as he ran, and recovered her great red leaf. But in the meantime twenty had hurried off in different directions with others just as good; and the little creature sat down and cried, and then, in a pet, sent a perfect pink snowstorm of petals from her tree, leaping from branch to branch, and stamping and shaking and pulling. At last, after another good cry, she chose the biggest she could find, and ran away laughing, to launch her boat amongst the rest.

But my attention was first and chiefly attracted by a group of fairies near the cottage, who were talking together around what seemed a last dying primrose. They talked singing, and their talk made a song, something like this:

"Sister Snowdrop died
  Before we were born."
"She came like a bride
  In a snowy morn."
"What's a bride?"
  "What is snow?
"Never tried."
  "Do not know."
"Who told you about her?"
  "Little Primrose there
Cannot do without her."
  "Oh, so sweetly fair!"
"Never fear,
  She will come,
Primrose dear."
  "Is she dumb?"

"She'll come by-and-by."
  "You will never see her."
"She went home to dies,
  "Till the new year."
"Snowdrop!" "'Tis no good
  To invite her."
"Primrose is very rude,
  "I will bite her."

"Oh, you naughty Pocket!

"Look, she drops her head."
"She deserved it, Rocket,
 "And she was nearly dead."
"To your hammock—off with you!"
 "And swing alone."
"No one will laugh with you."
 "No, not one."

"Now let us moan."
 "And cover her o'er."
"Primrose is gone."
 "All but the flower."
"Here is a leaf."
 "Lay her upon it."
"Follow in grief."
 "Pocket has done it."

"Deeper, poor creature!
 Winter may come."
"He cannot reach her—
 That is a hum."
"She is buried, the beauty!"
 "Now she is done."
"That was the duty."
 "Now for the fun."

And with a wild laugh they sprang away, most of them towards the cottage. During the latter part of the song-talk, they had formed themselves into a funeral procession, two of them bearing poor Primrose, whose death Pocket had hastened by biting her stalk, upon one of her own great leaves. They bore her solemnly along some distance, and then buried her under a tree. Although I say *her* I saw nothing but the withered primrose-flower on its long stalk. Pocket, who had been expelled from the company by common consent, went sulkily away towards her hammock, for she was the fairy of the calceolaria, and looked rather wicked. When she reached its stem, she stopped and looked round. I could not help speaking to her, for I stood near her. I said, "Pocket, how could you be so naughty?"

"I am never naughty," she said, half-crossly, half-defiantly; "only if you come near my hammock, I will bite you, and then you will go away."

"Why did you bite poor Primrose?"

"Because she said we should never see Snowdrop; as if we were not good enough to look at her, and she was, the proud thing!—served her right!"

"Oh, Pocket, Pocket," said I; but by this time the party which had gone towards the house, rushed out again, shouting and screaming with laughter. Half of them were on the cat's back, and half held on by her fur and tail, or ran beside her; till, more coming to their help, the furious cat was held fast; and they proceeded to pick the sparks out of her with thorns and pins, which they handled like harpoons. Indeed, there were more instruments at work about her than there could have been sparks in her. One little fellow who held on hard by the tip of the tail, with his feet planted on the ground at an angle of forty-five degrees, helping to keep her fast, administered a continuous flow of admonitions to Pussy.

"Now, Pussy, be patient. You know quite well it is all for your good. You cannot be comfortable with all those sparks in you; and, indeed, I am charitably disposed to believe" (here he became very pompous) "that they are the cause of all your bad temper; so we must have them all out, every one; else we shall be reduced to the painful necessity of cutting your claws, and pulling out your eye-teeth. Quiet! Pussy, quiet!"

But with a perfect hurricane of feline curses, the poor animal broke loose, and dashed across the garden and through the hedge, faster than even the fairies could follow. "Never mind, never mind, we shall find her again; and by that time she will have laid in a fresh stock of sparks. Hooray!" And off they set, after some new mischief.

But I will not linger to enlarge on the amusing display of these frolicsome creatures. Their manners and habits are now so well known to the world, having been so often described by eyewitnesses, that it would be only indulging self-conceit, to add my account in full to the rest. I cannot help wishing, however, that my readers could see them for themselves. Especially do I desire that they should see the fairy of the daisy; a little, chubby, round-eyed child, with such innocent trust in his look! Even the most mischievous of the fairies would not tease him, although he did not belong to their set at all, but was quite a little country bumpkin. He wandered about alone, and looked at everything, with his hands in his little pockets, and a white night-cap on, the darling! He was not so beautiful as many other wild flowers I saw afterwards, but so dear and loving in his looks and little confident ways.

17

CHAPTER IV
"When bale is att hyest, boote is nyest."
Ballad of Sir Aldingar.

By this time, my hostess was quite anxious that I should be gone. So, with warm thanks for their hospitality, I took my leave, and went my way through the little garden towards the forest. Some of the garden flowers had wandered into the wood, and were growing here and there along the path, but the trees soon became too thick and shadowy for them. I particularly noticed some tall lilies, which grew on both sides of the way, with large dazzlingly white flowers, set off by the universal green. It was now dark enough for me to see that every flower was shining with a light of its own. Indeed it was by this light that I saw them, an internal, peculiar light, proceeding from each, and not reflected from a common source of light as in the daytime. This light sufficed only for the plant itself, and was not strong enough to cast any but the faintest shadows around it, or to illuminate any of the neighbouring objects with other than the faintest tinge of its own individual hue. From the lilies above mentioned, from the campanulas, from the foxgloves, and every bell-shaped flower, curious little figures shot up their heads, peeped at me, and drew back. They seemed to inhabit them, as snails their shells but I was sure some of them were intruders, and belonged to the gnomes or goblin-fairies, who inhabit the ground and earthy creeping plants. From the cups of Arum lilies, creatures with great heads and grotesque faces shot up like Jack-in-the-box, and made grimaces at me; or rose slowly and slily over the edge of the cup, and spouted water at me, slipping suddenly back, like those little soldier-crabs that inhabit the shells of sea-snails. Passing a row of tall thistles, I saw them crowded with little faces, which peeped every one from behind its flower, and drew back as quickly; and I heard them saying to each other, evidently intending me to hear, but the speaker always hiding behind his tuft, when I looked in his direction, "Look at him! Look at him! He has begun a story without a beginning, and it will never have any end. He! he! he! Look at him!"

But as I went further into the wood, these sights and sounds became fewer, giving way to others of a different character. A little forest of wild hyacinths was alive with exquisite creatures, who stood nearly motionless, with drooping necks, holding each by the stem of her flower, and swaying gently with it, whenever a low breath of wind swung the crowded floral belfry. In like manner, though differing of course in form and meaning, stood a group of harebells, like little angels waiting, ready, till they were wanted to go on some yet unknown message. In darker nooks, by the mossy roots of the trees, or in little tufts of grass, each dwelling in a globe of its own green light, weaving a network of grass and its shadows, glowed the glowworms.

They were just like the glowworms of our own land, for they are fairies everywhere; worms in the day, and glowworms at night, when their own can appear, and they can be themselves to others as well as themselves. But they had their enemies here. For I saw great strong-armed beetles, hurrying about with most unwieldy haste, awkward as elephant-calves, looking apparently for glowworms; for the moment a beetle espied one, through what to it was a forest of grass, or an underwood of moss, it pounced upon it, and bore it away, in spite of its feeble resistance. Wondering what their object could be, I watched one of the beetles, and then I discovered a thing I could not account for. But it is no use trying to account for things in Fairy Land; and one who travels there soon learns to forget the very idea of doing so, and takes everything as it comes; like a child, who, being in a chronic condition of wonder, is surprised at nothing. What I saw was this. Everywhere, here and there over the ground, lay little, dark-looking lumps of something more like earth than anything else, and about the size of a chestnut. The beetles hunted in couples for these; and having found one, one of them stayed to watch it, while the other hurried to find a glowworm. By signals, I presume, between them, the latter soon found his companion again: they then took the glowworm and held its luminous tail to the dark earthly pellet; when lo, it shot up into the air like a sky-rocket, seldom, however, reaching the height of the highest tree. Just like a rocket too, it burst in the air, and fell in a shower of the most gorgeously coloured sparks of every variety of hue; golden and red, and purple and green, and blue and rosy fires crossed and inter-crossed each other, beneath the shadowy heads, and between the columnar stems of the forest trees. They never used the same glowworm twice, I observed; but let him go, apparently uninjured by the use they had made of him.

In other parts, the whole of the immediately surrounding foliage was illuminated by the interwoven dances in the air of splendidly coloured fire-flies, which sped hither and thither, turned, twisted, crossed, and recrossed, entwining every complexity of intervolved motion. Here and there, whole mighty trees glowed with an emitted phosphorescent light. You could trace the very course of the great roots in the earth by the faint light that came through; and every twig, and every vein on every leaf was a streak of pale fire.

All this time, as I went through the wood, I was haunted with the feeling that other shapes, more like my own size and mien, were moving about at a little distance on all sides of me. But as yet I could discern none of them, although the moon was high enough to send a great many of her rays down between the trees, and these rays were unusually bright, and sight-giving, notwithstanding she was only a half-moon. I constantly imagined, however, that forms were visible in all directions except that to which my gaze was turned; and that they only became invisible, or resolved themselves into other woodland shapes, the moment my looks were directed towards them. However this may have been, except for this feeling of presence, the woods seemed utterly bare of anything like human companionship, although my glance often fell on some object which I fancied to be a human form; for I soon found that I was quite deceived; as, the moment I fixed my regard on it, it showed plainly that it was a bush, or a tree, or a rock.

Soon a vague sense of discomfort possessed me. With variations of relief, this gradually increased; as if some evil thing were wandering about in my neighbourhood, sometimes nearer and sometimes further off, but still approaching. The feeling continued and deepened, until all my pleasure in the shows of various kinds that everywhere betokened the presence of the merry fairies vanished by degrees, and left me full of anxiety and fear, which I was unable to associate with any definite object whatever. At length the thought crossed my mind with horror: "Can it be possible that the Ash is looking for me? or that, in his nightly wanderings, his path is gradually verging towards mine?" I comforted myself, however, by remembering that he had started quite in another direction; one that would lead him, if he kept it, far apart from me; especially as, for the last two or three hours, I had been diligently journeying eastward. I kept on my way, therefore, striving by direct effort of the will against the encroaching fear; and to this end occupying my mind, as much as I could, with other thoughts. I was so far successful that, although I was conscious, if I yielded for a moment, I should be almost overwhelmed with horror, I was yet able to walk right on for an hour or more. What I feared I could not tell. Indeed, I was left in a state of the vaguest uncertainty as regarded the nature of my enemy, and knew not the mode or object of his attacks; for, somehow or other, none of my questions had succeeded in drawing a definite answer from the dame in the cottage. How then to defend myself I knew not; nor even by what sign I might with certainty recognise the presence of my foe; for as yet this vague though powerful fear was all the indication of danger I had. To add to my distress, the clouds in the west had risen nearly to the top of the skies, and they and the moon were travelling slowly towards each other. Indeed, some of their advanced guard had already met her, and she had begun to wade through a filmy vapour that gradually deepened.

At length she was for a moment almost entirely obscured. When she shone out again, with a brilliancy increased by the contrast, I saw plainly on the path before me—from around which at this spot the trees receded, leaving a small space of green sward—the shadow of a large hand, with knotty joints and protuberances here and there. Especially I remarked, even in the midst of my fear, the bulbous points of the fingers. I looked hurriedly all around, but could see nothing from which such a shadow should fall. Now, however, that I had a direction, however undetermined, in which to project my apprehension, the very sense of danger and need of action overcame that stifling which is the worst property of fear. I reflected in a moment, that if this were indeed a shadow, it was useless to look for the object that cast it in any other direction than between the shadow and the moon. I looked, and peered, and intensified my vision, all to no purpose. I could see nothing of that kind, not even an ash-tree in the neighbourhood. Still the shadow remained; not steady, but moving to and fro, and once I saw the fingers close, and grind themselves close, like the claws of a wild animal, as if in uncontrollable longing for some anticipated prey. There seemed but one mode left of discovering the substance of this shadow. I went forward boldly, though with an inward shudder which I would not heed, to the spot where the shadow lay, threw myself on the ground, laid my head within the form of the hand, and turned my eyes towards the moon Good heavens! what did I see? I wonder that ever I arose, and that the very shadow of the hand did not hold me where I lay until fear had frozen my brain. I saw the strangest figure; vague, shadowy, almost transparent, in the central parts, and gradually deepening in substance towards the outside, until it ended in extremities capable of casting such a shadow as fell from the hand, through the awful fingers of which I now saw the moon. The hand was uplifted in the attitude of a paw about to strike its prey. But the face, which throbbed with fluctuating and pulsatory visibility—not from changes in the light it reflected, but from changes in its own conditions of reflecting power, the alterations being from within, not from without—it was horrible. I do not know how to describe it. It caused a new sensation. Just as one cannot translate a horrible odour, or a ghastly pain, or a fearful sound, into words, so I cannot describe this new form of awful hideousness. I can only try to describe something that is not it, but seems somewhat parallel to it; or at least is suggested by it. It reminded me of what I had heard of vampires; for the face resembled that of a corpse more than anything else I can think of; especially when I can conceive such a face in motion, but not suggesting any life as the source of the motion. The features were rather handsome than otherwise, except the mouth, which had scarcely a curve in it. The lips were of equal thickness; but the thickness was not at all remarkable, even

21

although they looked slightly swollen. They seemed fixedly open, but were not wide apart. Of course I did not *remark* these lineaments at the time: I was too horrified for that. I noted them afterwards, when the form returned on my inward sight with a vividness too intense to admit of my doubting the accuracy of the reflex. But the most awful of the features were the eyes. These were alive, yet not with life.

They seemed lighted up with an infinite greed. A gnawing voracity, which devoured the devourer, seemed to be the indwelling and propelling power of the whole ghostly apparition. I lay for a few moments simply imbruted with terror; when another cloud, obscuring the moon, delivered me from the immediately paralysing effects of the presence to the vision of the object of horror, while it added the force of imagination to the power of fear within me; inasmuch as, knowing far worse cause for apprehension than before, I remained equally ignorant from what I had to defend myself, or how to take any precautions: he might be upon me in the darkness any moment. I sprang to my feet, and sped I knew not whither, only away from the spectre. I thought no longer of the path, and often narrowly escaped dashing myself against a tree, in my headlong flight of fear.

Great drops of rain began to patter on the leaves. Thunder began to mutter, then growl in the distance. I ran on. The rain fell heavier. At length the thick leaves could hold it up no longer; and, like a second firmament, they poured their torrents on the earth. I was soon drenched, but that was nothing. I came to a small swollen stream that rushed through the woods. I had a vague hope that if I crossed this stream, I should be in safety from my pursuer; but I soon found that my hope was as false as it was vague. I dashed across the stream, ascended a rising ground, and reached a more open space, where stood only great trees. Through them I directed my way, holding eastward as nearly as I could guess, but not at all certain that I was not moving in an opposite direction. My mind was just reviving a little from its extreme terror, when, suddenly, a flash of lightning, or rather a cataract of successive flashes, behind me, seemed to throw on the ground in front of me, but far more faintly than before, from the extent of the source of the light, the shadow of the same horrible hand. I sprang forward, stung to yet wilder speed; but had not run many steps before my foot slipped, and, vainly attempting to recover myself, I fell at the foot of one of the large trees. Half-stunned, I yet raised myself, and almost involuntarily looked back. All I saw was the hand within three feet of my face. But, at the same moment, I felt two large soft arms thrown round me from behind; and a voice like a woman's said: "Do not fear the goblin; he dares not hurt you now." With that, the hand was suddenly withdrawn as from a fire, and disappeared in the darkness and the rain. Overcome with the mingling of terror and joy, I lay for some time almost insensible. The first thing I remember is the sound of a voice above me, full and low, and strangely reminding me of the sound of a gentle wind amidst the leaves of a great tree. It murmured over and over again: "I may love him, I may love him; for he is a man, and I am only a beech-tree." I found I was seated on the ground, leaning against a human form, and supported still by the arms around me, which I knew to be those of a woman who must be rather above the human size, and largely proportioned. I turned my head, but without moving otherwise, for I feared lest the arms should untwine themselves; and clear, somewhat mournful eyes met mine. At least that is how they impressed me; but I could see very little of colour or outline as we sat in the dark and rainy shadow of the tree. The face seemed very lovely, and solemn from its stillness; with the aspect of one who is quite content, but waiting for something. I saw my conjecture from her arms was correct: she was above the human scale throughout, but not greatly.

"Why do you call yourself a beech-tree?" I said.

"Because I am one," she replied, in the same low, musical, murmuring voice.

"You are a woman," I returned.

"Do you think so? Am I very like a woman then?"

"You are a very beautiful woman. Is it possible you should not know it?"

"I am very glad you think so. I fancy I feel like a woman sometimes. I do so to-night—and always when the rain drips from my hair. For there is an old prophecy in our woods that one day we shall all be men and women like you. Do you know anything about it in your region? Shall I be very happy when I am a woman? I fear not, for it is always in nights like these that I feel like one. But I long to be a woman for all that."

I had let her talk on, for her voice was like a solution of all musical sounds. I now told her that I could hardly say whether women were happy or not. I knew one who had not been happy; and for my part, I had often longed for Fairy Land, as she now longed for the world of men. But then neither of us had lived long, and perhaps people grew happier as they grew older. Only I doubted it.

I could not help sighing. She felt the sigh, for her arms were still round me. She asked me how old I was.

"Twenty-one," said I.

"Why, you baby!" said she, and kissed me with the sweetest kiss of winds and odours. There was a cool faithfulness in the kiss that revived my heart wonderfully. I felt that I feared the dreadful Ash no more.

"What did the horrible Ash want with me?" I said.

"I am not quite sure, but I think he wants to bury you at the foot of his tree. But he shall not touch you, my child."

"Are all the ash-trees as dreadful as he?"

"Oh, no. They are all disagreeable selfish creatures—(what horrid men they will make, if it be true!)—but this one has a hole in his heart that nobody knows of but one or two; and he is always trying to fill it up, but he cannot. That must be what he wanted you for. I wonder if he will ever be a man. If he is, I hope they will kill him."

"How kind of you to save me from him!"

"I will take care that he shall not come near you again. But there are some in the wood more like me, from whom, alas! I cannot protect you. Only if you see any of them very beautiful, try to walk round them."

"What then?"

"I cannot tell you more. But now I must tie some of my hair about you, and then the Ash will not touch you. Here, cut some off. You men have strange cutting things about you."

She shook her long hair loose over me, never moving her arms.

"I cannot cut your beautiful hair. It would be a shame."

"Not cut my hair! It will have grown long enough before any is wanted again in this wild forest. Perhaps it may never be of any use again—not till I am a woman." And she sighed.

As gently as I could, I cut with a knife a long tress of flowing, dark hair, she hanging her beautiful head over me. When I had finished, she shuddered and breathed deep, as one does when an acute pain, steadfastly endured without sign of suffering, is at length relaxed. She then took the hair and tied it round me, singing a strange, sweet song, which I could not understand, but which left in me a feeling like this—

> *"I saw thee ne'er before;*
> *I see thee never more;*
> *But love, and help, and pain, beautiful one,*
> *Have made thee mine, till all my years are done."*

I cannot put more of it into words. She closed her arms about me again, and went on singing. The rain in the leaves, and a light wind that had arisen, kept her song company. I was wrapt in a trance of still delight. It told me the secret of the woods, and the flowers, and the birds. At one time I felt as if I was wandering in childhood through sunny spring forests, over carpets of primroses, anemones, and little white starry things—I had almost said creatures, and finding new wonderful flowers at every turn. At another, I lay half dreaming in the hot summer noon, with a book of old tales beside me, beneath a great beech; or, in autumn, grew sad because I trod on the leaves that had sheltered me, and received their last blessing in the sweet odours of decay; or, in a winter evening,

24

frozen still, looked up, as I went home to a warm fireside, through the netted boughs and twigs to the cold, snowy moon, with her opal zone around her. At last I had fallen asleep; for I know nothing more that passed till I found myself lying under a superb beech-tree, in the clear light of the morning, just before sunrise. Around me was a girdle of fresh beech-leaves. Alas! I brought nothing with me out of Fairy Land, but memories—memories. The great boughs of the beech hung drooping around me. At my head rose its smooth stem, with its great sweeps of curving surface that swelled like undeveloped limbs. The leaves and branches above kept on the song which had sung me asleep; only now, to my mind, it sounded like a farewell and a speedwell. I sat a long time, unwilling to go; but my unfinished story urged me on. I must act and wander. With the sun well risen, I rose, and put my arms as far as they would reach around the beech-tree, and kissed it, and said good-bye. A trembling went through the leaves; a few of the last drops of the night's rain fell from off them at my feet; and as I walked slowly away, I seemed to hear in a whisper once more the words: "I may love him, I may love him; for he is a man, and I am only a beech-tree."

CHAPTER V

"And she was smooth and full, as if one gush
Of life had washed her, or as if a sleep
Lay on her eyelid, easier to sweep
Than bee from daisy."
            BEDDOIS' Pygmalion.

"Sche was as whyt as lylye yn May,
Or snow that sneweth yn wynterys day."
            Romance of Sir Launfal.

I walked on, in the fresh morning air, as if new-born. The only thing that damped my pleasure was a cloud of something between sorrow and delight that crossed my mind with the frequently returning thought of my last night's hostess. "But then," thought I, "if she is sorry, I could not help it; and she has all the pleasures she ever had. Such a day as this is surely a joy to her, as much at least as to me. And her life will perhaps be the richer, for holding now within it the memory of what came, but could not stay. And if ever she is a woman, who knows but we may meet somewhere? there is plenty of room for meeting in the universe."

25

Comforting myself thus, yet with a vague compunction, as if I ought not to have left her, I went on. There was little to distinguish the woods to-day from those of my own land; except that all the wild things, rabbits, birds, squirrels, mice, and the numberless other inhabitants, were very tame; that is, they did not run away from me, but gazed at me as I passed, frequently coming nearer, as if to examine me more closely. Whether this came from utter ignorance, or from familiarity with the human appearance of beings who never hurt them, I could not tell. As I stood once, looking up to the splendid flower of a parasite, which hung from the branch of a tree over my head, a large white rabbit cantered slowly up, put one of its little feet on one of mine, and looked up at me with its red eyes, just as I had been looking up at the flower above me. I stooped and stroked it; but when I attempted to lift it, it banged the ground with its hind feet and scampered off at a great rate, turning, however, to look at me several times before I lost sight of it. Now and then, too, a dim human figure would appear and disappear, at some distance, amongst the trees, moving like a sleep-walker. But no one ever came near me.

This day I found plenty of food in the forest—strange nuts and fruits I had never seen before. I hesitated to eat them; but argued that, if I could live on the air of Fairy Land, I could live on its food also. I found my reasoning correct, and the result was better than I had hoped; for it not only satisfied my hunger, but operated in such a way upon my senses that I was brought into far more complete relationship with the things around me. The human forms appeared much more dense and defined; more tangibly visible, if I may say so. I seemed to know better which direction to choose when any doubt arose. I began to feel in some degree what the birds meant in their songs, though I could not express it in words, any more than you can some landscapes. At times, to my surprise, I found myself listening attentively, and as if it were no unusual thing with me, to a conversation between two squirrels or monkeys. The subjects were not very interesting, except as associated with the individual life and necessities of the little creatures: where the best nuts were to be found in the neighbourhood, and who could crack them best, or who had most laid up for the winter, and such like; only they never said where the store was. There was no great difference in kind between their talk and our ordinary human conversation. Some of the creatures I never heard speak at all, and believe they never do so, except under the impulse of some great excitement. The mice talked; but the hedgehogs seemed very phlegmatic; and though I met a couple of moles above ground several times, they never said a word to each other in my hearing. There were no wild beasts in the forest; at least, I did not see one larger than a wild cat. There were plenty of snakes, however, and I do not think they were all harmless; but none ever bit me.

Soon after mid-day I arrived at a bare rocky hill, of no great size, but very steep; and having no trees—scarcely even a bush—upon it, entirely exposed to the heat of the sun. Over this my way seemed to lie, and I immediately began the ascent. On reaching the top, hot and weary, I looked around me, and saw that the forest still stretched as far as the sight could reach on every side of me. I observed that the trees, in the direction in which I was about to descend, did not come so near the foot of the hill as on the other side, and was especially regretting the unexpected postponement of shelter, because this side of the hill seemed more difficult to descend than the other had been to climb, when my eye caught the appearance of a natural path, winding down through broken rocks and along the course of a tiny stream, which I hoped would lead me more easily to the foot. I tried it, and found the descent not at all laborious; nevertheless, when I reached the bottom, I was very tired and exhausted with the heat. But just where the path seemed to end, rose a great rock, quite overgrown with shrubs and creeping plants, some of them in full and splendid blossom: these almost concealed an opening in the rock, into which the path appeared to lead. I entered, thirsting for the shade which it promised. What was my delight to find a rocky cell, all the angles rounded away with rich moss, and every ledge and projection crowded with lovely ferns, the variety of whose forms, and groupings, and shades wrought in me like a poem; for such a harmony could not exist, except they all consented to some one end! A little well of the clearest water filled a mossy hollow in one corner. I drank, and felt as if I knew what the elixir of life must be; then threw myself on a mossy mound that lay like a couch along the inner end. Here I lay in a delicious reverie for some time; during which all lovely forms, and colours, and sounds seemed to use my brain as a common hall, where they could come and go, unbidden and unexcused. I had never imagined that such capacity for simple happiness lay in me, as was now awakened by this assembly of forms and spiritual sensations, which yet were far too vague to admit of being translated into any shape common to my own and another mind. I had lain for an hour, I should suppose, though it may have been far longer, when, the harmonious tumult in my mind having somewhat relaxed, I became aware that my eyes were fixed on a strange, time-worn bas-relief on the rock opposite to me. This, after some pondering, I concluded to represent Pygmalion, as he awaited the quickening of his statue. The sculptor sat more rigid than the figure to which his eyes were turned. That seemed about to step from its pedestal and embrace the man, who waited rather than expected.

"A lovely story," I said to myself. "This cave, now, with the bushes cut away from the entrance to let the light in, might be such a place as he would choose, withdrawn from the notice of men, to set up his block of marble, and mould into a visible body the thought already clothed with form in the unseen hall of the sculptor's brain. And, indeed, if I mistake not," I said, starting up, as a sudden ray of light arrived at that moment through a crevice in the roof, and lighted up a small portion of the rock, bare of vegetation, "this very rock is marble, white enough and delicate enough for any statue, even if destined to become an ideal woman in the arms of the sculptor."

I took my knife and removed the moss from a part of the block on which I had been lying; when, to my surprise, I found it more like alabaster than ordinary marble, and soft to the edge of the knife. In fact, it was alabaster. By an inexplicable, though by no means unusual kind of impulse, I went on removing the moss from the surface of the stone; and soon saw that it was polished, or at least smooth, throughout. I continued my labour; and after clearing a space of about a couple of square feet, I observed what caused me to prosecute the work with more interest and care than before. For the ray of sunlight had now reached the spot I had cleared, and under its lustre the alabaster revealed its usual slight transparency when polished, except where my knife had scratched the surface; and I observed that the transparency seemed to have a definite limit, and to end upon an opaque body like the more solid, white marble. I was careful to scratch no more. And first, a vague anticipation gave way to a startling sense of possibility; then, as I proceeded, one revelation after another produced the entrancing conviction, that under the crust of alabaster lay a dimly visible form in marble, but whether of man or woman I could not yet tell. I worked on as rapidly as the necessary care would permit; and when I had uncovered the whole mass, and rising from my knees, had retreated a little way, so that the effect of the whole might fall on me, I saw before me with sufficient plainness— though at the same time with considerable indistinctness, arising from the limited amount of light the place admitted, as well as from the nature of the object itself—a block of pure alabaster enclosing the form, apparently in marble, of a reposing woman. She lay on one side, with her hand under her cheek, and her face towards me; but her hair had fallen partly over her face, so that I could not see the expression of the whole. What I did see appeared to me perfectly lovely; more near the face that had been born with me in my soul, than anything I had seen before in nature or art. The actual outlines of the rest of the form were so indistinct, that the more than semi-opacity of the alabaster seemed insufficient to account for the fact; and I conjectured that a light robe added its obscurity. Numberless histories passed through my mind of change of substance from enchantment and other causes, and of imprisonments such as this before me. I thought of the Prince of the Enchanted City, half marble and half a man; of Ariel; of Niobe; of the Sleeping Beauty in the Wood; of the bleeding trees; and many other histories. Even my adventure of the preceding evening with the lady of the beech-tree contributed to arouse the wild hope, that by some means life might be given to this form also, and that, breaking from her alabaster tomb, she might glorify my eyes with her presence. "For," I argued, "who can tell but this cave may be the home of Marble, and this, essential Marble— that spirit of marble which, present throughout, makes it capable of being moulded into any form? Then if she should awake! But how to awake her? A kiss awoke the Sleeping Beauty! a kiss cannot reach her through the incrusting alabaster." I kneeled, however, and kissed the pale coffin; but she slept on. I bethought me of Orpheus, and the following stones—that trees should follow his music seemed nothing surprising now. Might not a song awake this form, that the glory of motion might for a time displace the loveliness of rest? Sweet sounds can go where kisses may not enter. I sat and thought. Now, although always delighting in music, I had never been gifted with the power of song, until I entered the fairy forest. I had a voice, and I had a true sense of sound; but when I tried to sing, the one would not content the other, and so I remained silent. This morning, however, I had found myself, ere I was aware, rejoicing in a song; but whether it was before or after I had eaten of the fruits of the forest, I could not satisfy myself. I concluded it was after, however; and that the increased impulse to sing I now felt, was in part owing to having drunk of the little well, which shone like a brilliant eye in a corner of the cave. I sat down on the ground by the "antenatal tomb," leaned upon it with my face towards the head of the figure within, and sang—the words and tones coming together, and inseparably connected, as if word and tone formed one thing; or, as if each word could be uttered only in that tone, and was incapable of distinction from it, except in idea, by an acute analysis. I sang something like this: but the words are only a dull representation of a state whose very elevation precluded the possibility of remembrance; and in which I presume the words really employed were as far above these, as that state transcended this wherein I recall it:

"Marble woman, vainly sleeping
In the very death of dreams!
Wilt thou—slumber from thee sweeping,
All but what with vision teems—
Hear my voice come through the golden
Mist of memory and hope;

And with shadowy smile embolden
Me with primal Death to cope?

"Thee the sculptors all pursuing,
Have embodied but their own;
Round their visions, form enduring,
Marble vestments thou hast thrown;
But thyself, in silence winding,
Thou hast kept eternally;
Thee they found not, many finding—
I have found thee: wake for me."

As I sang, I looked earnestly at the face so vaguely revealed before me. I fancied, yet believed it to be but fancy, that through the dim veil of the alabaster, I saw a motion of the head as if caused by a sinking sigh. I gazed more earnestly, and concluded that it was but fancy. Neverthless I could not help singing again—

"Rest is now filled full of beauty,
And can give thee up, I ween;
Come thou forth, for other duty
Motion pineth for her queen.

"Or, if needing years to wake thee
From thy slumbrous solitudes,
Come, sleep-walking, and betake thee
To the friendly, sleeping woods.

Sweeter dreams are in the forest,
Round thee storms would never rave;
And when need of rest is sorest,
Glide thou then into thy cave.

"Or, if still thou choosest rather
Marble, be its spell on me;
Let thy slumber round me gather,
Let another dream with thee!"

Again I paused, and gazed through the stony shroud, as if, by very force of penetrative sight, I would clear every lineament of the lovely face. And now I thought the hand that had lain under the cheek, had slipped a little downward. But then I could not be sure that I had at first observed its position accurately. So I sang again; for the longing had grown into a

30

passionate need of seeing her alive—

> *"Or art thou Death, O woman? for since I*
> *Have set me singing by thy side,*
> *Life hath forsook the upper sky,*
> *And all the outer world hath died.*

> *"Yea, I am dead; for thou hast drawn*
> *My life all downward unto thee.*
> *Dead moon of love! let twilight dawn:*
> *Awake! and let the darkness flee.*

> *"Cold lady of the lovely stone!*
> *Awake! or I shall perish here;*
> *And thou be never more alone,*
> *My form and I for ages near.*

> *"But words are vain; reject them all—*
> *They utter but a feeble part:*
> *Hear thou the depths from which they call,*
> *The voiceless longing of my heart."*

There arose a slightly crashing sound. Like a sudden apparition that comes and is gone, a white form, veiled in a light robe of whiteness, burst upwards from the stone, stood, glided forth, and gleamed away towards the woods. For I followed to the mouth of the cave, as soon as the amazement and concentration of delight permitted the nerves of motion again to act; and saw the white form amidst the trees, as it crossed a little glade on the edge of the forest where the sunlight fell full, seeming to gather with intenser radiance on the one object that floated rather than flitted through its lake of beams. I gazed after her in a kind of despair; found, freed, lost! It seemed useless to follow, yet follow I must. I marked the direction she took; and without once looking round to the forsaken cave, I hastened towards the forest.

CHAPTER VI

"Ah, let a man beware, when his wishes, fulfilled, rain down
upon him, and his happiness is unbounded."
—FOUQUE, Der Zauberring.

"Thy red lips, like worms,
Travel over my cheek."
      —MOTHERWELL.

But as I crossed the space between the foot of the hill and the forest, a vision of another kind delayed my steps. Through an opening to the westward flowed, like a stream, the rays of the setting sun, and overflowed with a ruddy splendour the open space where I was. And riding as it were down this stream towards me, came a horseman in what appeared red armour. From frontlet to tail, the horse likewise shone red in the sunset. I felt as if I must have seen the knight before; but as he drew near, I could recall no feature of his countenance. Ere he came up to me, however, I remembered the legend of Sir Percival in the rusty armour, which I had left unfinished in the old book in the cottage: it was of Sir Percival that he reminded me. And no wonder; for when he came close up to me, I saw that, from crest to heel, the whole surface of his armour was covered with a light rust. The golden spurs shone, but the iron greaves glowed in the sunlight. The *morning star*, which hung from his wrist, glittered and glowed with its silver and bronze. His whole appearance was terrible; but his face did not answer to this appearance. It was sad, even to gloominess; and something of shame seemed to cover it. Yet it was noble and high, though thus beclouded; and the form looked lofty, although the head drooped, and the whole frame was bowed as with an inward grief. The horse seemed to share in his master's dejection, and walked spiritless and slow. I noticed, too, that the white plume on his helmet was discoloured and drooping. "He has fallen in a joust with spears," I said to myself; "yet it becomes not a noble knight to be conquered in spirit because his body hath fallen." He appeared not to observe me, for he was riding past without looking up, and started into a warlike attitude the moment the first sound of my voice reached him. Then a flush, as of shame, covered all of his face that the lifted beaver disclosed. He returned my greeting with distant courtesy, and passed on. But suddenly, he reined up, sat a moment still, and then turning his horse, rode back to where I stood looking after him.
"I am ashamed," he said, "to appear a knight, and in such a guise; but it behoves me to tell you to take warning from me, lest the same evil, in his kind, overtake the singer that has befallen the knight. Hast thou ever read the story of Sir Percival and the"—(here he shuddered, that his armour rang)—"Maiden of the Alder-tree?"
"In part, I have," said I; "for yesterday, at the entrance of this forest, I found in a cottage the volume wherein it is recorded." "Then take heed," he rejoined; "for, see my armour—I put it off; and as it befell to him, so

32

has it befallen to me. I that was proud am humble now. Yet is she terribly beautiful—beware. Never," he added, raising his head, "shall this armour be furbished, but by the blows of knightly encounter, until the last speck has disappeared from every spot where the battle-axe and sword of evil-doers, or noble foes, might fall; when I shall again lift my head, and say to my squire, 'Do thy duty once more, and make this armour shine.'"

Before I could inquire further, he had struck spurs into his horse and galloped away, shrouded from my voice in the noise of his armour. For I called after him, anxious to know more about this fearful enchantress; but in vain—he heard me not. "Yet," I said to myself, "I have now been often warned; surely I shall be well on my guard; and I am fully resolved I shall not be ensnared by any beauty, however beautiful. Doubtless, some one man may escape, and I shall be he." So I went on into the wood, still hoping to find, in some one of its mysterious recesses, my lost lady of the marble. The sunny afternoon died into the loveliest twilight. Great bats began to flit about with their own noiseless flight, seemingly purposeless, because its objects are unseen. The monotonous music of the owl issued from all unexpected quarters in the half-darkness around me. The glow-worm was alight here and there, burning out into the great universe. The night-hawk heightened all the harmony and stillness with his oft-recurring, discordant jar. Numberless unknown sounds came out of the unknown dusk; but all were of twilight-kind, oppressing the heart as with a condensed atmosphere of dreamy undefined love and longing. The odours of night arose, and bathed me in that luxurious mournfulness peculiar to them, as if the plants whence they floated had been watered with bygone tears. Earth drew me towards her bosom; I felt as if I could fall down and kiss her. I forgot I was in Fairy Land, and seemed to be walking in a perfect night of our own old nursing earth. Great stems rose about me, uplifting a thick multitudinous roof above me of branches, and twigs, and leaves—the bird and insect world uplifted over mine, with its own landscapes, its own thickets, and paths, and glades, and dwellings; its own bird-ways and insect-delights. Great boughs crossed my path; great roots based the tree-columns, and mightily clasped the earth, strong to lift and strong to uphold. It seemed an old, old forest, perfect in forest ways and pleasures. And when, in the midst of this ecstacy, I remembered that under some close canopy of leaves, by some giant stem, or in some mossy cave, or beside some leafy well, sat the lady of the marble, whom my songs had called forth into the outer world, waiting (might it not be?) to meet and thank her deliverer in a twilight which would veil her confusion, the whole night became one dream-realm of joy, the central form of which was everywhere present, although unbeheld. Then, remembering how my songs seemed to have called her from the marble, piercing through the pearly shroud of alabaster—"Why," thought I, "should not my voice reach her now, through the ebon night that inwraps her." My voice burst into song so spontaneously that it seemed involuntarily.

> *"Not a sound*
> *But, echoing in me,*
> *Vibrates all around*
> *With a blind delight,*
> *Till it breaks on Thee,*
> *Queen of Night!*
>
> *Every tree,*
> *O'ershadowing with gloom,*
> *Seems to cover thee*
> *Secret, dark, love-still'd,*
> *In a holy room*
> *Silence-filled.*
>
> *"Let no moon*
> *Creep up the heaven to-night;*
> *I in darksome noon*
> *Walking hopefully,*
> *Seek my shrouded light—*
> *Grope for thee!*
>
> *"Darker grow*
> *The borders of the dark!*
> *Through the branches glow,*
> *From the roof above,*
> *Star and diamond-sparks*
> *Light for love."*

Scarcely had the last sounds floated away from the hearing of my own ears, when I heard instead a low delicious laugh near me. It was not the laugh of one who would not be heard, but the laugh of one who has just received something long and patiently desired—a laugh that ends in a low musical moan. I started, and, turning sideways, saw a dim white figure seated beside an intertwining thicket of smaller trees and underwood.

"It is my white lady!" I said, and flung myself on the ground beside her; striving, through the gathering darkness, to get a glimpse of the form which had broken its marble prison at my call.

"It is your white lady!" said the sweetest voice, in reply, sending a thrill of speechless delight through a heart which all the love-charms of the preceding day and evening had been tempering for this culminating hour. Yet, if I would have confessed it, there was something either in the sound of the voice, although it seemed sweetness itself, or else in this yielding which awaited no gradation of gentle approaches, that did not vibrate harmoniously with the beat of my inward music. And likewise, when, taking her hand in mine, I drew closer to her, looking for the beauty of her face, which, indeed, I found too plenteously, a cold shiver ran through me; but "it is the marble," I said to myself, and heeded it not. She withdrew her hand from mine, and after that would scarce allow me to touch her. It seemed strange, after the fulness of her first greeting, that she could not trust me to come close to her. Though her words were those of a lover, she kept herself withdrawn as if a mile of space interposed between us.

"Why did you run away from me when you woke in the cave?" I said.

"Did I?" she returned. "That was very unkind of me; but I did not know better."

"I wish I could see you. The night is very dark."

"So it is. Come to my grotto. There is light there."

"Have you another cave, then?"

"Come and see."

But she did not move until I rose first, and then she was on her feet before I could offer my hand to help her. She came close to my side, and conducted me through the wood. But once or twice, when, involuntarily almost, I was about to put my arm around her as we walked on through the warm gloom, she sprang away several paces, always keeping her face full towards me, and then stood looking at me, slightly stooping, in the attitude of one who fears some half-seen enemy. It was too dark to discern the expression of her face. Then she would return and walk close beside me again, as if nothing had happened. I thought this strange; but, besides that I had almost, as I said before, given up the attempt to account for appearances in Fairy Land, I judged that it would be very unfair to expect from one who had slept so long and had been so suddenly awakened, a behaviour correspondent to what I might unreflectingly look for. I knew not what she might have been dreaming about. Besides, it was possible that, while her words were free, her sense of touch might be exquisitely delicate.

At length, after walking a long way in the woods, we arrived at another thicket, through the intertexture of which was glimmering a pale rosy light.

"Push aside the branches," she said, "and make room for us to enter."
I did as she told me.
"Go in," she said; "I will follow you."
I did as she desired, and found myself in a little cave, not very unlike the marble cave. It was festooned and draperied with all kinds of green that cling to shady rocks. In the furthest corner, half-hidden in leaves, through which it glowed, mingling lovely shadows between them, burned a bright rosy flame on a little earthen lamp. The lady glided round by the wall from behind me, still keeping her face towards me, and seated herself in the furthest corner, with her back to the lamp, which she hid completely from my view. I then saw indeed a form of perfect loveliness before me. Almost it seemed as if the light of the rose-lamp shone through her (for it could not be reflected from her); such a delicate shade of pink seemed to shadow what in itself must be a marbly whiteness of hue. I discovered afterwards, however, that there was one thing in it I did not like; which was, that the white part of the eye was tinged with the same slight roseate hue as the rest of the form. It is strange that I cannot recall her features; but they, as well as her somewhat girlish figure, left on me simply and only the impression of intense loveliness. I lay down at her feet, and gazed up into her face as I lay. She began, and told me a strange tale, which, likewise, I cannot recollect; but which, at every turn and every pause, somehow or other fixed my eyes and thoughts upon her extreme beauty; seeming always to culminate in something that had a relation, revealed or hidden, but always operative, with her own loveliness. I lay entranced. It was a tale which brings back a feeling as of snows and tempests; torrents and water-sprites; lovers parted for long, and meeting at last; with a gorgeous summer night to close up the whole. I listened till she and I were blended with the tale; till she and I were the whole history. And we had met at last in this same cave of greenery, while the summer night hung round us heavy with love, and the odours that crept through the silence from the sleeping woods were the only signs of an outer world that invaded our solitude. What followed I cannot clearly remember. The succeeding horror almost obliterated it. I woke as a grey dawn stole into the cave. The damsel had disappeared; but in the shrubbery, at the mouth of the cave, stood a strange horrible object. It looked like an open coffin set up on one end; only that the part for the head and neck was defined from the shoulder-part. In fact, it was a rough representation of the human frame, only hollow, as if made of decaying bark torn from a tree.
It had arms, which were only slightly seamed, down from the shoulder-blade by the elbow, as if the bark had healed again from the cut of a knife. But the arms moved, and the hand and the fingers were tearing

asunder a long silky tress of hair. The thing turned round—it had for a face and front those of my enchantress, but now of a pale greenish hue in the light of the morning, and with dead lustreless eyes. In the horror of the moment, another fear invaded me. I put my hand to my waist, and found indeed that my girdle of beech-leaves was gone. Hair again in her hands, she was tearing it fiercely. Once more, as she turned, she laughed a low laugh, but now full of scorn and derision; and then she said, as if to a companion with whom she had been talking while I slept, "There he is; you can take him now." I lay still, petrified with dismay and fear; for I now saw another figure beside her, which, although vague and indistinct, I yet recognised but too well. It was the Ash-tree. My beauty was the Maid of the Alder! and she was giving me, spoiled of my only availing defence, into the hands of my awful foe. The Ash bent his Gorgon-head, and entered the cave. I could not stir. He drew near me. His ghoul-eyes and his ghastly face fascinated me. He came stooping, with the hideous hand outstretched, like a beast of prey. I had given myself up to a death of unfathomable horror, when, suddenly, and just as he was on the point of seizing me, the dull, heavy blow of an axe echoed through the wood, followed by others in quick repetition. The Ash shuddered and groaned, withdrew the outstretched hand, retreated backwards to the mouth of the cave, then turned and disappeared amongst the trees. The other walking Death looked at me once, with a careless dislike on her beautifully moulded features; then, heedless any more to conceal her hollow deformity, turned her frightful back and likewise vanished amid the green obscurity without. I lay and wept. The Maid of the Alder-tree had befooled me—nearly slain me—in spite of all the warnings I had received from those who knew my danger.

CHAPTER VII

"Fight on, my men, Sir Andrew sayes,
A little I am hurt, but yett not slaine;
I'le but lye downe and bleede awhile,
And then I'le rise and fight againe."
Ballad of Sir Andrew Barton.

But I could not remain where I was any longer, though the daylight was hateful to me, and the thought of the great, innocent, bold sunrise unendurable. Here there was no well to cool my face, smarting with the bitterness of my own tears. Nor would I have washed in the well of that

37

grotto, had it flowed clear as the rivers of Paradise. I rose, and feebly left the sepulchral cave. I took my way I knew not whither, but still towards the sunrise. The birds were singing; but not for me. All the creatures spoke a language of their own, with which I had nothing to do, and to which I cared not to find the key any more.

I walked listlessly along. What distressed me most—more even than my own folly—was the perplexing question, How can beauty and ugliness dwell so near? Even with her altered complexion and her face of dislike; disenchanted of the belief that clung around her; known for a living, walking sepulchre, faithless, deluding, traitorous; I felt notwithstanding all this, that she was beautiful. Upon this I pondered with undiminished perplexity, though not without some gain. Then I began to make surmises as to the mode of my deliverance; and concluded that some hero, wandering in search of adventure, had heard how the forest was infested; and, knowing it was useless to attack the evil thing in person, had assailed with his battle-axe the body in which he dwelt, and on which he was dependent for his power of mischief in the wood. "Very likely," I thought, "the repentant-knight, who warned me of the evil which has befallen me, was busy retrieving his lost honour, while I was sinking into the same sorrow with himself; and, hearing of the dangerous and mysterious being, arrived at his tree in time to save me from being dragged to its roots, and buried like carrion, to nourish him for yet deeper insatiableness." I found afterwards that my conjecture was correct. I wondered how he had fared when his blows recalled the Ash himself, and that too I learned afterwards.

I walked on the whole day, with intervals of rest, but without food; for I could not have eaten, had any been offered me; till, in the afternoon, I seemed to approach the outskirts of the forest, and at length arrived at a farm-house. An unspeakable joy arose in my heart at beholding an abode of human beings once more, and I hastened up to the door, and knocked. A kind-looking, matronly woman, still handsome, made her appearance; who, as soon as she saw me, said kindly, "Ah, my poor boy, you have come from the wood! Were you in it last night?"

I should have ill endured, the day before, to be called *boy*; but now the motherly kindness of the word went to my heart; and, like a boy indeed, I burst into tears. She soothed me right gently; and, leading me into a room, made me lie down on a settle, while she went to find me some refreshment. She soon returned with food, but I could not eat. She almost compelled me to swallow some wine, when I revived sufficiently to be able to answer some of her questions. I told her the whole story.

"It is just as I feared," she said; "but you are now for the night beyond the reach of any of these dreadful creatures. It is no wonder they could delude a child like you. But I must beg you, when my husband comes in, not to say a word about these things; for he thinks me even half crazy for believing anything of the sort. But I must believe my senses, as he cannot believe beyond his, which give him no intimations of this kind. I think he could spend the whole of Midsummer-eve in the wood and come back with the report that he saw nothing worse than himself. Indeed, good man, he would hardly find anything better than himself, if he had seven more senses given him."

"But tell me how it is that she could be so beautiful without any heart at all—without any place even for a heart to live in."

"I cannot quite tell," she said; "but I am sure she would not look so beautiful if she did not take means to make herself look more beautiful than she is. And then, you know, you began by being in love with her before you saw her beauty, mistaking her for the lady of the marble—another kind altogether, I should think. But the chief thing that makes her beautiful is this: that, although she loves no man, she loves the love of any man; and when she finds one in her power, her desire to bewitch him and gain his love (not for the sake of his love either, but that she may be conscious anew of her own beauty, through the admiration he manifests), makes her very lovely—with a self-destructive beauty, though; for it is that which is constantly wearing her away within, till, at last, the decay will reach her face, and her whole front, when all the lovely mask of nothing will fall to pieces, and she be vanished for ever. So a wise man, whom she met in the wood some years ago, and who, I think, for all his wisdom, fared no better than you, told me, when, like you, he spent the next night here, and recounted to me his adventures."

I thanked her very warmly for her solution, though it was but partial; wondering much that in her, as in woman I met on my first entering the forest, there should be such superiority to her apparent condition. Here she left me to take some rest; though, indeed, I was too much agitated to rest in any other way than by simply ceasing to move.

In half an hour, I heard a heavy step approach and enter the house. A jolly voice, whose slight huskiness appeared to proceed from overmuch laughter, called out "Betsy, the pigs' trough is quite empty, and that is a pity. Let them swill, lass! They're of no use but to get fat. Ha! ha! ha! Gluttony is not forbidden in their commandments. Ha! ha! ha!" The very voice, kind and jovial, seemed to disrobe the room of the strange look which all new places wear—to disenchant it out of the realm of the ideal into that of the actual. It began to look as if I had known every corner of it for twenty years; and when, soon after, the dame came and fetched me to partake of their early supper, the grasp of his great hand, and the harvest-moon of his benevolent face, which was needed to light up the rotundity of the globe beneath it, produced such a reaction in me, that, for a moment, I could hardly believe that there was a Fairy Land; and that all I had passed through since I left home, had not been the wandering dream of a diseased imagination, operating on a too mobile frame, not merely causing me indeed to travel, but peopling for me with vague phantoms the regions through which my actual steps had led me. But the next moment my eye fell upon a little girl who was sitting in the chimney-corner, with a little book open on her knee, from which she had apparently just looked up to fix great inquiring eyes upon me. I believed in Fairy Land again. She went on with her reading, as soon as she saw that I observed her looking at me. I went near, and peeping over her shoulder, saw that she was reading *The History of Graciosa and Percinet*. "Very improving book, sir," remarked the old farmer, with a good-humoured laugh. "We are in the very hottest corner of Fairy Land here. Ha! ha! Stormy night, last night, sir."

"Was it, indeed?" I rejoined. "It was not so with me. A lovelier night I never saw." "Indeed! Where were you last night?"

"I spent it in the forest. I had lost my way."

"Ah! then, perhaps, you will be able to convince my good woman, that there is nothing very remarkable about the forest; for, to tell the truth, it bears but a bad name in these parts. I dare say you saw nothing worse than yourself there?"

"I hope I did," was my inward reply; but, for an audible one, I contented myself with saying, "Why, I certainly did see some appearances I could hardly account for; but that is nothing to be wondered at in an unknown wild forest, and with the uncertain light of the moon alone to go by."

"Very true! you speak like a sensible man, sir. We have but few sensible folks round about us. Now, you would hardly credit it, but my wife believes every fairy-tale that ever was written. I cannot account for it. She is a most sensible woman in everything else."

"But should not that make you treat her belief with something of respect, though you cannot share in it yourself?"

"Yes, that is all very well in theory; but when you come to live every day in the midst of absurdity, it is far less easy to behave respectfully to it. Why, my wife actually believes the story of the 'White Cat.' You know it, I dare say."

"I read all these tales when a child, and know that one especially well."

"But, father," interposed the little girl in the chimney-corner, "you know quite well that mother is descended from that very princess who was changed by the wicked fairy into a white cat. Mother has told me so a many times, and you ought to believe everything she says."

"I can easily believe that," rejoined the farmer, with another fit of laughter; "for, the other night, a mouse came gnawing and scratching beneath the floor, and would not let us go to sleep. Your mother sprang out of bed, and going as near it as she could, mewed so infernally like a great cat, that the noise ceased instantly. I believe the poor mouse died of the fright, for we have never heard it again. Ha! ha! ha!"

The son, an ill-looking youth, who had entered during the conversation, joined in his father's laugh; but his laugh was very different from the old man's: it was polluted with a sneer. I watched him, and saw that, as soon as it was over, he looked scared, as if he dreaded some evil consequences to follow his presumption. The woman stood near, waiting till we should seat ourselves at the table, and listening to it all with an amused air, which had something in it of the look with which one listens to the sententious remarks of a pompous child. We sat down to supper, and I ate heartily. My bygone distresses began already to look far off.

"In what direction are you going?" asked the old man.

"Eastward," I replied; nor could I have given a more definite answer. "Does the forest extend much further in that direction?"

"Oh! for miles and miles; I do not know how far. For although I have lived on the borders of it all my life, I have been too busy to make journeys of discovery into it. Nor do I see what I could discover. It is only trees and trees, till one is sick of them. By the way, if you follow the eastward track from here, you will pass close to what the children say is the very house of the ogre that Hop-o'-my-Thumb visited, and ate his little daughters with the crowns of gold."

"Oh, father! ate his little daughters! No; he only changed their gold crowns for nightcaps; and the great long-toothed ogre killed them in mistake; but I do not think even he ate them, for you know they were his own little ogresses."

"Well, well, child; you know all about it a great deal better than I do. However, the house has, of course, in such a foolish neighbourhood as this, a bad enough name; and I must confess there is a woman living in it, with teeth long enough, and white enough too, for the lineal descendant of the greatest ogre that ever was made. I think you had better not go near her."

In such talk as this the night wore on. When supper was finished, which lasted some time, my hostess conducted me to my chamber.

"If you had not had enough of it already," she said, "I would have put you in another room, which looks towards the forest; and where you would most likely have seen something more of its inhabitants. For they frequently pass the window, and even enter the room sometimes. Strange creatures spend whole nights in it, at certain seasons of the year. I am used to it, and do not mind it. No more does my little girl, who sleeps in it always. But this room looks southward towards the open country, and they never show themselves here; at least I never saw any."

I was somewhat sorry not to gather any experience that I might have, of the inhabitants of Fairy Land; but the effect of the farmer's company, and of my own later adventures, was such, that I chose rather an undisturbed night in my more human quarters; which, with their clean white curtains and white linen, were very inviting to my weariness.

In the morning I awoke refreshed, after a profound and dreamless sleep. The sun was high, when I looked out of the window, shining over a wide, undulating, cultivated country. Various garden-vegetables were growing beneath my window. Everything was radiant with clear sunlight. The dew-drops were sparkling their busiest; the cows in a near-by field were eating as if they had not been at it all day yesterday; the maids were singing at their work as they passed to and fro between the out-houses: I did not believe in Fairy Land. I went down, and found the family already at breakfast. But before I entered the room where they sat, the little girl came to me, and looked up in my face, as though she wanted to say something to me. I stooped towards her; she put her arms round my neck, and her mouth to my ear, and whispered—

"A white lady has been flitting about the house all night."

"No whispering behind doors!" cried the farmer; and we entered together. "Well, how have you slept? No bogies, eh?"

"Not one, thank you; I slept uncommonly well."

"I am glad to hear it. Come and breakfast."

After breakfast, the farmer and his son went out; and I was left alone with the mother and daughter.

"When I looked out of the window this morning," I said, "I felt almost certain that Fairy Land was all a delusion of my brain; but whenever I come near you or your little daughter, I feel differently. Yet I could persuade myself, after my last adventures, to go back, and have nothing more to do with such strange beings."

"How will you go back?" said the woman.

"Nay, that I do not know."

"Because I have heard, that, for those who enter Fairy Land, there is no way of going back. They must go on, and go through it. How, I do not in the least know."

"That is quite the impression on my own mind. Something compels me to go on, as if my only path was onward, but I feel less inclined this morning to continue my adventures."

"Will you come and see my little child's room? She sleeps in the one I told you of, looking towards the forest."

"Willingly," I said.

So we went together, the little girl running before to open the door for us. It was a large room, full of old-fashioned furniture, that seemed to have once belonged to some great house.

The window was built with a low arch, and filled with lozenge-shaped panes. The wall was very thick, and built of solid stone. I could see that part of the house had been erected against the remains of some old castle or abbey, or other great building; the fallen stones of which had probably served to complete it. But as soon as I looked out of the window, a gush of wonderment and longing flowed over my soul like the tide of a great sea. Fairy Land lay before me, and drew me towards it with an irresistible attraction. The trees bathed their great heads in the waves of the morning, while their roots were planted deep in gloom; save where on the borders the sunshine broke against their stems, or swept in long streams through their avenues, washing with brighter hue all the leaves over which it flowed; revealing the rich brown of the decayed leaves and fallen pine-cones, and the delicate greens of the long grasses and tiny forests of moss that covered the channel over which it passed in motionless rivers of light. I turned hurriedly to bid my hostess farewell without further delay. She smiled at my haste, but with an anxious look.

"You had better not go near the house of the ogre, I think. My son will show you into another path, which will join the first beyond it."

Not wishing to be headstrong or too confident any more, I agreed; and having taken leave of my kind entertainers, went into the wood, accompanied by the youth. He scarcely spoke as we went along; but he led me through the trees till we struck upon a path. He told me to follow it, and, with a muttered "good morning" left me.

CHAPTER VIII

"I am a part of the part, which at first was the whole."
GOETHE.—Mephistopheles in Faust.

My spirits rose as I went deeper; into the forest; but I could not regain my former elasticity of mind. I found cheerfulness to be like life itself—not to be created by any argument. Afterwards I learned, that the best way to manage some kinds of pain filled thoughts, is to dare them to do their worst; to let them lie and gnaw at your heart till they are tired; and you find you still have a residue of life they cannot kill. So, better and worse, I went on, till I came to a little clearing in the forest. In the middle of this clearing stood a long, low hut, built with one end against a single tall cypress, which rose like a spire to the building. A vague misgiving crossed my mind when I saw it; but I must needs go closer, and look through a little half-open door, near the opposite end from the cypress. Window I saw none. On peeping in, and looking towards the further end, I saw a lamp burning, with a dim, reddish flame, and the head of a woman, bent downwards, as if reading by its light. I could see nothing more for a few moments. At length, as my eyes got used to the dimness of the place, I saw that the part of the rude building near me was used for household purposes; for several rough utensils lay here and there, and a bed stood in the corner.

An irresistible attraction caused me to enter. The woman never raised her face, the upper part of which alone I could see distinctly; but, as soon as I stepped within the threshold, she began to read aloud, in a low and not altogether unpleasing voice, from an ancient little volume which she held open with one hand on the table upon which stood the lamp. What she read was something like this:

"So, then, as darkness had no beginning, neither will it ever have an end. So, then, is it eternal. The negation of aught else, is its affirmation. Where the light cannot come, there abideth the darkness. The light doth but hollow a mine out of the infinite extension of the darkness. And ever upon the steps of the light treadeth the darkness; yea, springeth in fountains and wells amidst it, from the secret channels of its mighty sea. Truly, man is but a passing flame, moving unquietly amid the surrounding rest of night; without which he yet could not be, and whereof he is in part compounded."

As I drew nearer, and she read on, she moved a little to turn a leaf of the dark old volume, and I saw that her face was sallow and slightly forbidding. Her forehead was high, and her black eyes repressedly quiet. But she took no notice of me. This end of the cottage, if cottage it could be called, was destitute of furniture, except the table with the lamp, and the chair on which the woman sat. In one corner was a door, apparently of a cupboard in the wall, but which might lead to a room beyond. Still the irresistible desire which had made me enter the building urged me: I must open that door, and see what was beyond it. I approached, and laid my hand on the rude latch. Then the woman spoke, but without lifting her head or looking at me: "You had better not open that door." This was uttered quite quietly; and she went on with her reading, partly in silence, partly aloud; but both modes seemed equally intended for herself alone. The prohibition, however, only increased my desire to see; and as she took no further notice, I gently opened the door to its full width, and looked in. At first, I saw nothing worthy of attention. It seemed a common closet, with shelves on each hand, on which stood various little necessaries for the humble uses of a cottage. In one corner stood one or two brooms, in another a hatchet and other common tools; showing that it was in use every hour of the day for household purposes. But, as I looked, I saw that there were no shelves at the back, and that an empty space went in further; its termination appearing to be a faintly glimmering wall or curtain, somewhat less, however, than the width and height of the doorway where I stood. But, as I continued looking, for a few seconds, towards this faintly luminous limit, my eyes came into true relation with their object. All at once, with such a shiver as when one is suddenly conscious of the presence of another in a room where he has, for hours, considered himself alone, I saw that the seemingly luminous extremity was a sky, as of night, beheld through the long perspective of a narrow, dark passage, through what, or built of what, I could not tell. As I gazed, I clearly discerned two or three stars glimmering faintly in the distant blue. But, suddenly, and as if it had been running fast from a far distance for this very point, and had turned the corner without abating its swiftness, a dark figure sped into and along the passage from the blue opening at the remote end. I started back and shuddered, but kept looking, for I could not help it. On and on it came, with a speedy approach but delayed arrival; till, at last, through the many gradations of approach, it seemed to come within the sphere of myself, rushed up to me, and passed me into the cottage. All I could tell of its appearance was, that it seemed to be a dark human figure. Its motion was entirely noiseless, and might be called a gliding, were it not that it appeared that of a runner, but with ghostly feet. I had moved back yet a little to let him pass me, and looked round after him instantly. I could not see him.

"Where is he?" I said, in some alarm, to the woman, who still sat reading. "There, on the floor, behind you," she said, pointing with her arm half-outstretched, but not lifting her eyes. I turned and looked, but saw nothing. Then with a feeling that there was yet something behind me, I looked round over my shoulder; and there, on the ground, lay a black shadow, the size of a man. It was so dark, that I could see it in the dim light of the lamp, which shone full upon it, apparently without thinning at all the intensity of its hue.

"I told you," said the woman, "you had better not look into that closet."

"What is it?" I said, with a growing sense of horror.

"It is only your shadow that has found you," she replied. "Everybody's shadow is ranging up and down looking for him. I believe you call it by a different name in your world: yours has found you, as every person's is almost certain to do who looks into that closet, especially after meeting one in the forest, whom I dare say you have met."

Here, for the first time, she lifted her head, and looked full at me: her mouth was full of long, white, shining teeth; and I knew that I was in the house of the ogre. I could not speak, but turned and left the house, with the shadow at my heels. "A nice sort of valet to have," I said to myself bitterly, as I stepped into the sunshine, and, looking over my shoulder, saw that it lay yet blacker in the full blaze of the sunlight. Indeed, only when I stood between it and the sun, was the blackness at all diminished. I was so bewildered—stunned—both by the event itself and its suddenness, that I could not at all realise to myself what it would be to have such a constant and strange attendance; but with a dim conviction that my present dislike would soon grow to loathing, I took my dreary way through the wood.

CHAPTER IX

"O lady! we receive but what we give,
And in our life alone does nature live:
Ours is her wedding garments ours her shrorwd!

. . . . .

Ah! from the soul itself must issue forth,
A light, a glory, a fair luminous cloud,
Enveloping the Earth—
And from the soul itself must there be sent
A sweet and potent voice of its own birth,
Of all sweet sounds the life and element!"
              COLERIDGE.

From this time, until I arrived at the palace of Fairy Land, I can attempt no consecutive account of my wanderings and adventures. Everything, henceforward, existed for me in its relation to my attendant. What influence he exercised upon everything into contact with which I was brought, may be understood from a few detached instances. To begin with this very day on which he first joined me: after I had walked heartlessly along for two or three hours, I was very weary, and lay down to rest in a most delightful part of the forest, carpeted with wild flowers. I lay for half an hour in a dull repose, and then got up to pursue my way. The flowers on the spot where I had lain were crushed to the earth: but I saw that they would soon lift their heads and rejoice again in the sun and air. Not so those on which my shadow had lain. The very outline of it could be traced in the withered lifeless grass, and the scorched and shrivelled flowers which stood there, dead, and hopeless of any resurrection. I shuddered, and hastened away with sad forebodings.

In a few days, I had reason to dread an extension of its baleful influences from the fact, that it was no longer confined to one position in regard to myself. Hitherto, when seized with an irresistible desire to look on my evil demon (which longing would unaccountably seize me at any moment, returning at longer or shorter intervals, sometimes every minute), I had to turn my head backwards, and look over my shoulder; in which position, as long as I could retain it, I was fascinated. But one day, having come out on a clear grassy hill, which commanded a glorious prospect, though of what I cannot now tell, my shadow moved round, and came in front of me. And, presently, a new manifestation increased my distress. For it began to coruscate, and shoot out on all sides a radiation of dim shadow. These rays of gloom issued from the central shadow as from a black sun, lengthening and shortening with continual change. But wherever a ray struck, that part of earth, or sea, or sky, became void, and desert, and sad to my heart. On this, the first development of its new power, one ray shot out beyond the rest, seeming to lengthen infinitely, until it smote the great sun on the face, which withered and darkened beneath the blow. I turned away and went on. The shadow retreated to its former position; and when I looked again, it had drawn in all its spears of darkness, and followed like a dog at my heels.

Once, as I passed by a cottage, there came out a lovely fairy child, with two wondrous toys, one in each hand. The one was the tube through which the fairy-gifted poet looks when he beholds the same thing everywhere; the other that through which he looks when he combines into new forms of loveliness those images of beauty which his own choice has gathered from all regions wherein he has travelled. Round the child's head was an aureole of emanating rays. As I looked at him in wonder and delight, round crept from behind me the something dark, and the child stood in my shadow. Straightway he was a commonplace boy, with a rough broad-brimmed straw hat, through which brim the sun shone from behind. The toys he carried were a multiplying-glass and a kaleidoscope. I sighed and departed.

One evening, as a great silent flood of western gold flowed through an avenue in the woods, down the stream, just as when I saw him first, came the sad knight, riding on his chestnut steed.

But his armour did not shine half so red as when I saw him first.

Many a blow of mighty sword and axe, turned aside by the strength of his mail, and glancing adown the surface, had swept from its path the fretted rust, and the glorious steel had answered the kindly blow with the thanks of returning light. These streaks and spots made his armour look like the floor of a forest in the sunlight. His forehead was higher than before, for the contracting wrinkles were nearly gone; and the sadness that remained on his face was the sadness of a dewy summer twilight, not that of a frosty autumn morn. He, too, had met the Alder-maiden as I, but he had plunged into the torrent of mighty deeds, and the stain was nearly washed away. No shadow followed him. He had not entered the dark house; he had not had time to open the closet door. "Will he ever look in?" I said to myself. "*Must* his shadow find him some day?" But I could not answer my own questions.

We travelled together for two days, and I began to love him. It was plain that he suspected my story in some degree; and I saw him once or twice looking curiously and anxiously at my attendant gloom, which all this time had remained very obsequiously behind me; but I offered no explanation, and he asked none. Shame at my neglect of his warning, and a horror which shrunk from even alluding to its cause, kept me silent; till, on the evening of the second day, some noble words from my companion roused all my heart; and I was at the point of falling on his neck, and telling him the whole story; seeking, if not for helpful advice, for of that I was hopeless, yet for the comfort of sympathy—when round slid the shadow and inwrapt my friend; and I could not trust him.

The glory of his brow vanished; the light of his eye grew cold; and I held my peace. The next morning we parted.

But the most dreadful thing of all was, that I now began to feel something like satisfaction in the presence of the shadow. I began to be rather vain of my attendant, saying to myself, "In a land like this, with so many illusions everywhere, I need his aid to disenchant the things around me. He does away with all appearances, and shows me things in their true colour and form. And I am not one to be fooled with the vanities of the common crowd. I will not see beauty where there is none. I will dare to behold things as they are. And if I live in a waste instead of a paradise, I will live knowing where I live." But of this a certain exercise of his power which soon followed quite cured me, turning my feelings towards him once more into loathing and distrust. It was thus:

One bright noon, a little maiden joined me, coming through the wood in a direction at right angles to my path. She came along singing and dancing, happy as a child, though she seemed almost a woman. In her hands—now in one, now in another—she carried a small globe, bright and clear as the purest crystal. This seemed at once her plaything and her greatest treasure. At one moment, you would have thought her utterly careless of it, and at another, overwhelmed with anxiety for its safety. But I believe she was taking care of it all the time, perhaps not least when least occupied about it. She stopped by me with a smile, and bade me good day with the sweetest voice. I felt a wonderful liking to the child—for she produced on me more the impression of a child, though my understanding told me differently. We talked a little, and then walked on together in the direction I had been pursuing. I asked her about the globe she carried, but getting no definite answer, I held out my hand to take it. She drew back, and said, but smiling almost invitingly the while, "You must not touch it;"—then, after a moment's pause—"Or if you do, it must be very gently." I touched it with a finger. A slight vibratory motion arose in it, accompanied, or perhaps manifested, by a faint sweet sound. I touched it again, and the sound increased. I touched it the third time: a tiny torrent of harmony rolled out of the little globe. She would not let me touch it any more.

We travelled on together all that day. She left me when twilight came on; but next day, at noon, she met me as before, and again we travelled till evening. The third day she came once more at noon, and we walked on together. Now, though we had talked about a great many things connected with Fairy Land, and the life she had led hitherto, I had never been able to learn anything about the globe. This day, however, as we went on, the shadow glided round and inwrapt the maiden. It could not change her. But my desire to know about the globe, which in his gloom began to waver as with an inward light, and to shoot out flashes of many-coloured flame, grew irresistible. I put out both my hands and laid hold of it. It began to sound as before. The sound rapidly increased, till it grew a low tempest of harmony, and the globe trembled, and quivered, and throbbed between my hands. I had not the heart to pull it away from the maiden, though I held it in spite of her attempts to take it from me; yes, I shame to say, in spite of her prayers, and, at last, her tears. The music went on growing in, intensity and complication of tones, and the globe vibrated and heaved; till at last it burst in our hands, and a black vapour broke upwards from out of it; then turned, as if blown sideways, and enveloped the maiden, hiding even the shadow in its blackness. She held fast the fragments, which I abandoned, and fled from me into the forest in the direction whence she had come, wailing like a child, and crying, "You have broken my globe; my globe is broken—my globe is broken!" I followed her, in the hope of comforting her; but had not pursued her far, before a sudden cold gust of wind bowed the tree-tops above us, and swept through their stems around us; a great cloud overspread the day, and a fierce tempest came on, in which I lost sight of her. It lies heavy on my heart to this hour. At night, ere I fall asleep, often, whatever I may be thinking about, I suddenly hear her voice, crying out, "You have broken my globe; my globe is broken; ah, my globe!"

Here I will mention one more strange thing; but whether this peculiarity was owing to my shadow at all, I am not able to assure myself. I came to a village, the inhabitants of which could not at first sight be distinguished from the dwellers in our land. They rather avoided than sought my company, though they were very pleasant when I addressed them. But at last I observed, that whenever I came within a certain distance of any one of them, which distance, however, varied with different individuals, the whole appearance of the person began to change; and this change increased in degree as I approached. When I receded to the former distance, the former appearance was restored. The nature of the change was grotesque, following no fixed rule. The nearest resemblance to it that I know, is the distortion produced in your countenance when you look at it as reflected in a concave or convex surface—say, either side of a bright spoon. Of this phenomenon I first became aware in rather a ludicrous way. My host's daughter was a very pleasant pretty girl, who made herself more agreeable to me than most of those about me. For some days my companion-shadow had been less obtrusive than usual; and such was the reaction of spirits occasioned by the simple mitigation of torment, that, although I had cause enough besides to be gloomy, I felt light and comparatively happy. My impression is, that she was quite aware of the law of appearances that existed between the people of the place and myself, and had resolved to amuse herself at my expense; for one evening, after some jesting and raillery, she, somehow or other, provoked me to attempt to kiss her. But she was well defended from any assault of the kind. Her countenance became, of a sudden, absurdly hideous; the pretty mouth was elongated and otherwise amplified sufficiently to have allowed of six simultaneous kisses. I started back in bewildered dismay; she burst into the merriest fit of laughter, and ran from the room. I soon found that the same undefinable law of change operated between me and all the other villagers; and that, to feel I was in pleasant company, it was absolutely necessary for me to discover and observe the right focal distance between myself and each one with whom I had to do. This done, all went pleasantly enough. Whether, when I happened to neglect this precaution, I presented to them an equally ridiculous appearance, I did not ascertain; but I presume that the alteration was common to the approximating parties. I was likewise unable to determine whether I was a necessary party to the production of this strange transformation, or whether it took place as well, under the given circumstances, between the inhabitants themselves.

CHAPTER X

"From Eden's bowers the full-fed rivers flow,
To guide the outcasts to the land of woe:
Our Earth one little toiling streamlet yields.
To guide the wanderers to the happy fields."

After leaving this village, where I had rested for nearly a week, I travelled through a desert region of dry sand and glittering rocks, peopled principally by goblin-fairies. When I first entered their domains, and, indeed, whenever I fell in with another tribe of them, they began mocking me with offered handfuls of gold and jewels, making hideous grimaces at me, and performing the most antic homage, as if they thought I expected reverence, and meant to humour me like a maniac. But ever, as soon as one cast his eyes on the shadow behind me, he made a wry face, partly of pity, partly of contempt, and looked ashamed, as if he had been caught doing something inhuman; then, throwing down his handful of gold, and ceasing all his grimaces, he stood aside to let me pass in peace, and made signs to his companions to do the like. I had no inclination to observe them much, for the shadow was in my heart as well as at my heels. I walked listlessly and almost hopelessly along, till I arrived one day at a small spring; which, bursting cool from the heart of a sun-heated rock, flowed somewhat southwards from the direction I had been taking. I drank of this spring, and found myself wonderfully refreshed. A kind of love to the cheerful little stream arose in my heart. It was born in a desert; but it seemed to say to itself, "I will flow, and sing, and lave my banks, till I make my desert a paradise." I thought I could not do better than follow it, and see what it made of it. So down with the stream I went, over rocky lands, burning with sunbeams. But the rivulet flowed not far, before a few blades of grass appeared on its banks, and then, here and there, a stunted bush. Sometimes it disappeared altogether under ground; and after I had wandered some distance, as near as I could guess, in the direction it seemed to take, I would suddenly hear it again, singing, sometimes far away to my right or left, amongst new rocks, over which it made new cataracts of watery melodies. The verdure on its banks increased as it flowed; other streams joined it; and at last, after many days' travel, I found myself, one gorgeous summer evening, resting by the side of a broad river, with a glorious horse-chestnut tree towering above me, and dropping its blossoms, milk-white and rosy-red, all about me. As I sat, a gush of joy sprang forth in my heart, and over flowed at my eyes.

Through my tears, the whole landscape glimmered in such bewildering loveliness, that I felt as if I were entering Fairy Land for the first time, and some loving hand were waiting to cool my head, and a loving word to warm my heart. Roses, wild roses, everywhere! So plentiful were they, they not only perfumed the air, they seemed to dye it a faint rose-hue. The colour floated abroad with the scent, and clomb, and spread, until the whole west blushed and glowed with the gathered incense of roses. And my heart fainted with longing in my bosom.

Could I but see the Spirit of the Earth, as I saw once the in dwelling woman of the beech-tree, and my beauty of the pale marble, I should be content. Content!—Oh, how gladly would I die of the light of her eyes! Yea, I would cease to be, if that would bring me one word of love from the one mouth. The twilight sank around, and infolded me with sleep. I slept as I had not slept for months. I did not awake till late in the morning; when, refreshed in body and mind, I rose as from the death that wipes out the sadness of life, and then dies itself in the new morrow. Again I followed the stream; now climbing a steep rocky bank that hemmed it in; now wading through long grasses and wild flowers in its path; now through meadows; and anon through woods that crowded down to the very lip of the water.

At length, in a nook of the river, gloomy with the weight of overhanging foliage, and still and deep as a soul in which the torrent eddies of pain have hollowed a great gulf, and then, subsiding in violence, have left it full of a motionless, fathomless sorrow—I saw a little boat lying. So still was the water here, that the boat needed no fastening. It lay as if some one had just stepped ashore, and would in a moment return. But as there were no signs of presence, and no track through the thick bushes; and, moreover, as I was in Fairy Land where one does very much as he pleases, I forced my way to the brink, stepped into the boat, pushed it, with the help of the tree-branches, out into the stream, lay down in the bottom, and let my boat and me float whither the stream would carry us. I seemed to lose myself in the great flow of sky above me unbroken in its infinitude, except when now and then, coming nearer the shore at a bend in the river, a tree would sweep its mighty head silently above mine, and glide away back into the past, never more to fling its shadow over me. I fell asleep in this cradle, in which mother Nature was rocking her weary child; and while I slept, the sun slept not, but went round his arched way. When I awoke, he slept in the waters, and I went on my silent path beneath a round silvery moon. And a pale moon looked up from the floor of the great blue cave that lay in the abysmal silence beneath.

Why are all reflections lovelier than what we call the reality?—not so grand or so strong, it may be, but always lovelier? Fair as is the gliding sloop on the shining sea, the wavering, trembling, unresting sail below is fairer still. Yea, the reflecting ocean itself, reflected in the mirror, has a wondrousness about its waters that somewhat vanishes when I turn towards itself. All mirrors are magic mirrors. The commonest room is a room in a poem when I turn to the glass. (And this reminds me, while I write, of a strange story which I read in the fairy palace, and of which I will try to make a feeble memorial in its place.) In whatever way it may be accounted for, of one thing we may be sure, that this feeling is no cheat; for there is no cheating in nature and the simple unsought feelings of the soul. There must be a truth involved in it, though we may but in part lay hold of the meaning. Even the memories of past pain are beautiful; and past delights, though beheld only through clefts in the grey clouds of sorrow, are lovely as Fairy Land. But how have I wandered into the deeper fairyland of the soul, while as yet I only float towards the fairy palace of Fairy Land! The moon, which is the lovelier memory or reflex of the down-gone sun, the joyous day seen in the faint mirror of the brooding night, had rapt me away.

I sat up in the boat. Gigantic forest trees were about me; through which, like a silver snake, twisted and twined the great river. The little waves, when I moved in the boat, heaved and fell with a plash as of molten silver, breaking the image of the moon into a thousand morsels, fusing again into one, as the ripples of laughter die into the still face of joy. The sleeping woods, in undefined massiveness; the water that flowed in its sleep; and, above all, the enchantress moon, which had cast them all, with her pale eye, into the charmed slumber, sank into my soul, and I felt as if I had died in a dream, and should never more awake.

From this I was partly aroused by a glimmering of white, that, through the trees on the left, vaguely crossed my vision, as I gazed upwards. But the trees again hid the object; and at the moment, some strange melodious bird took up its song, and sang, not an ordinary bird-song, with constant repetitions of the same melody, but what sounded like a continuous strain, in which one thought was expressed, deepening in intensity as evolved in progress. It sounded like a welcome already overshadowed with the coming farewell. As in all sweetest music, a tinge of sadness was in every note. Nor do we know how much of the pleasures even of life we owe to the intermingled sorrows. Joy cannot unfold the deepest truths, although deepest truth must be deepest joy. Cometh white-robed Sorrow, stooping and wan, and flingeth wide the doors she may not enter. Almost we linger with Sorrow for very love.

As the song concluded the stream bore my little boat with a gentle sweep round a bend of the river; and lo! on a broad lawn, which rose from the water's edge with a long green slope to a clear elevation from which the trees receded on all sides, stood a stately palace glimmering ghostly in the moonshine: it seemed to be built throughout of the whitest marble. There was no reflection of moonlight from windows—there seemed to be none; so there was no cold glitter; only, as I said, a ghostly shimmer. Numberless shadows tempered the shine, from column and balcony and tower. For everywhere galleries ran along the face of the buildings; wings were extended in many directions; and numberless openings, through which the moonbeams vanished into the interior, and which served both for doors and windows, had their separate balconies in front, communicating with a common gallery that rose on its own pillars. Of course, I did not discover all this from the river, and in the moonlight. But, though I was there for many days, I did not succeed in mastering the inner topography of the building, so extensive and complicated was it.

Here I wished to land, but the boat had no oars on board. However, I found that a plank, serving for a seat, was unfastened, and with that I brought the boat to the bank and scrambled on shore. Deep soft turf sank beneath my feet, as I went up the ascent towards the palace.

When I reached it, I saw that it stood on a great platform of marble, with an ascent, by broad stairs of the same, all round it. Arrived on the platform, I found there was an extensive outlook over the forest, which, however, was rather veiled than revealed by the moonlight.

Entering by a wide gateway, but without gates, into an inner court, surrounded on all sides by great marble pillars supporting galleries above, I saw a large fountain of porphyry in the middle, throwing up a lofty column of water, which fell, with a noise as of the fusion of all sweet sounds, into a basin beneath; overflowing which, it ran into a single channel towards the interior of the building. Although the moon was by this time so low in the west, that not a ray of her light fell into the court, over the height of the surrounding buildings; yet was the court lighted by a second reflex from the sun of other lands. For the top of the column of water, just as it spread to fall, caught the moonbeams, and like a great pale lamp, hung high in the night air, threw a dim memory of light (as it were) over the court below. This court was paved in diamonds of white and red marble. According to my custom since I entered Fairy Land, of taking for a guide whatever I first found moving in any direction, I followed the stream from the basin of the fountain. It led me to a great open door, beneath the ascending steps of which it ran through a low arch and disappeared. Entering here, I found myself in a great hall, surrounded with white pillars, and paved with black and white. This I could see by the moonlight, which, from the other side, streamed through open windows into the hall.

Its height I could not distinctly see. As soon as I entered, I had the feeling so common to me in the woods, that there were others there besides myself, though I could see no one, and heard no sound to indicate a presence. Since my visit to the Church of Darkness, my power of seeing the fairies of the higher orders had gradually diminished, until it had almost ceased. But I could frequently believe in their presence while unable to see them. Still, although I had company, and doubtless of a safe kind, it seemed rather dreary to spend the night in an empty marble hall, however beautiful, especially as the moon was near the going down, and it would soon be dark. So I began at the place where I entered, and walked round the hall, looking for some door or passage that might lead me to a more hospitable chamber. As I walked, I was deliciously haunted with the feeling that behind some one of the seemingly innumerable pillars, one who loved me was waiting for me. Then I thought she was following me from pillar to pillar as I went along; but no arms came out of the faint moonlight, and no sigh assured me of her presence.

At length I came to an open corridor, into which I turned; notwithstanding that, in doing so, I left the light behind. Along this I walked with outstretched hands, groping my way, till, arriving at another corridor, which seemed to strike off at right angles to that in which I was, I saw at the end a faintly glimmering light, too pale even for moonshine, resembling rather a stray phosphorescence. However, where everything was white, a little light went a great way. So I walked on to the end, and a long corridor it was. When I came up to the light, I found that it proceeded from what looked like silver letters upon a door of ebony; and, to my surprise even in the home of wonder itself, the letters formed the words, *The Chamber of Sir Anodos*. Although I had as yet no right to the honours of a knight, I ventured to conclude that the chamber was indeed intended for me; and, opening the door without hesitation, I entered. Any doubt as to whether I was right in so doing, was soon dispelled. What to my dark eyes seemed a blaze of light, burst upon me. A fire of large pieces of some sweet-scented wood, supported by dogs of silver, was burning on the hearth, and a bright lamp stood on a table, in the midst of a plentiful meal, apparently awaiting my arrival. But what surprised me more than all, was, that the room was in every respect a copy of my own room, the room whence the little stream from my basin had led me into Fairy Land. There was the very carpet of grass and moss and daisies, which I had myself designed; the curtains of pale blue silk, that fell like a cataract over the windows; the old-fashioned bed, with the chintz furniture, on which I had slept from boyhood. "Now I shall sleep," I said to myself. "My shadow dares not come here."

I sat down to the table, and began to help myself to the good things before me with confidence. And now I found, as in many instances before, how true the fairy tales are; for I was waited on, all the time of my meal, by invisible hands. I had scarcely to do more than look towards anything I wanted, when it was brought me, just as if it had come to me of itself. My glass was kept filled with the wine I had chosen, until I looked towards another bottle or decanter; when a fresh glass was substituted, and the other wine supplied. When I had eaten and drank more heartily and joyfully than ever since I entered Fairy Land, the whole was removed by several attendants, of whom some were male and some female, as I thought I could distinguish from the way the dishes were lifted from the table, and the motion with which they were carried out of the room. As soon as they were all taken away, I heard a sound as of the shutting of a door, and knew that I was left alone. I sat long by the fire, meditating, and wondering how it would all end; and when at length, wearied with thinking, I betook myself to my own bed, it was half with a hope that, when I awoke in the morning, I should awake not only in my own room, but in my own castle also; and that I should walk, out upon my own native soil, and find that Fairy Land was, after all, only a vision of the night. The sound of the falling waters of the fountain floated me into oblivion.

CHAPTER XI

"A wilderness of building, sinking far
And self-withdrawn into a wondrous depth,
Far sinking into splendour—without end:
Fabric it seemed of diamond and of gold,
With alabaster domes, and silver spires,
And blazing terrace upon terrace, high
Uplifted."
                    WORDSWORTH.

But when, after a sleep, which, although dreamless, yet left behind it a sense of past blessedness, I awoke in the full morning, I found, indeed, that the room was still my own; but that it looked abroad upon an unknown landscape of forest and hill and dale on the one side—and on the other, upon the marble court, with the great fountain, the crest of which now flashed glorious in the sun, and cast on the pavement beneath a shower of faint shadows from the waters that fell from it into the marble basin below.

Agreeably to all authentic accounts of the treatment of travellers in Fairy Land, I found by my bedside a complete suit of fresh clothing, just such as I was in the habit of wearing; for, though varied sufficiently from the one removed, it was yet in complete accordance with my tastes. I dressed myself in this, and went out. The whole palace shone like silver in the sun. The marble was partly dull and partly polished; and every pinnacle, dome, and turret ended in a ball, or cone, or cusp of silver. It was like frost-work, and too dazzling, in the sun, for earthly eyes like mine.

I will not attempt to describe the environs, save by saying, that all the pleasures to be found in the most varied and artistic arrangement of wood and river, lawn and wild forest, garden and shrubbery, rocky hill and luxurious vale; in living creatures wild and tame, in gorgeous birds, scattered fountains, little streams, and reedy lakes—all were here. Some parts of the palace itself I shall have occasion to describe more minutely.

For this whole morning I never thought of my demon shadow; and not till the weariness which supervened on delight brought it again to my memory, did I look round to see if it was behind me: it was scarcely discernible. But its presence, however faintly revealed, sent a pang to my heart, for the pain of which, not all the beauties around me could compensate. It was followed, however, by the comforting reflection that, peradventure, I might here find the magic word of power to banish the demon and set me free, so that I should no longer be a man beside myself. The Queen of Fairy Land, thought I, must dwell here: surely she will put forth her power to deliver me, and send me singing through the further gates of her country back to my own land. "Shadow of me!" I said; "which art not me, but which representest thyself to me as me; here I may find a shadow of light which will devour thee, the shadow of darkness! Here I may find a blessing which will fall on thee as a curse, and damn thee to the blackness whence thou hast emerged unbidden." I said this, stretched at length on the slope of the lawn above the river; and as the hope arose within me, the sun came forth from a light fleecy cloud that swept across his face; and hill and dale, and the great river winding on through the still mysterious forest, flashed back his rays as with a silent shout of joy; all nature lived and glowed; the very earth grew warm beneath me; a magnificent dragon-fly went past me like an arrow from a bow, and a whole concert of birds burst into choral song.

The heat of the sun soon became too intense even for passive support. I therefore rose, and sought the shelter of one of the arcades. Wandering along from one to another of these, wherever my heedless steps led me, and wondering everywhere at the simple magnificence of the building, I arrived at another hall, the roof of which was of a pale blue, spangled with constellations of silver stars, and supported by porphyry pillars of a paler red than ordinary.—In this house (I may remark in passing), silver seemed everywhere preferred to gold; and such was the purity of the air, that it showed nowhere signs of tarnishing.—The whole of the floor of this hall, except a narrow path behind the pillars, paved with black, was hollowed into a huge basin, many feet deep, and filled with the purest, most liquid and radiant water. The sides of the basin were white marble, and the bottom was paved with all kinds of refulgent stones, of every shape and hue.

In their arrangement, you would have supposed, at first sight, that there was no design, for they seemed to lie as if cast there from careless and playful hands; but it was a most harmonious confusion; and as I looked at the play of their colours, especially when the waters were in motion, I came at last to feel as if not one little pebble could be displaced, without injuring the effect of the whole. Beneath this floor of the water, lay the reflection of the blue inverted roof, fretted with its silver stars, like a second deeper sea, clasping and upholding the first. The fairy bath was probably fed from the fountain in the court. Led by an irresistible desire, I undressed, and plunged into the water. It clothed me as with a new sense and its object both in one. The waters lay so close to me, they seemed to enter and revive my heart. I rose to the surface, shook the water from my hair, and swam as in a rainbow, amid the coruscations of the gems below seen through the agitation caused by my motion. Then, with open eyes, I dived, and swam beneath the surface. And here was a new wonder. For the basin, thus beheld, appeared to extend on all sides like a sea, with here and there groups as of ocean rocks, hollowed by ceaseless billows into wondrous caves and grotesque pinnacles. Around the caves grew sea-weeds of all hues, and the corals glowed between; while far off, I saw the glimmer of what seemed to be creatures of human form at home in the waters. I thought I had been enchanted; and that when I rose to the surface, I should find myself miles from land, swimming alone upon a heaving sea; but when my eyes emerged from the waters, I saw above me the blue spangled vault, and the red pillars around. I dived again, and found myself once more in the heart of a great sea. I then arose, and swam to the edge, where I got out easily, for the water reached the very brim, and, as I drew near washed in tiny waves over the black marble border. I dressed, and went out, deeply refreshed.

And now I began to discern faint, gracious forms, here and there throughout the building. Some walked together in earnest conversation. Others strayed alone. Some stood in groups, as if looking at and talking about a picture or a statue. None of them heeded me. Nor were they plainly visible to my eyes. Sometimes a group, or single individual, would fade entirely out of the realm of my vision as I gazed. When evening came, and the moon arose, clear as a round of a horizon-sea when the sun hangs over it in the west, I began to see them all more plainly; especially when they came between me and the moon; and yet more especially, when I myself was in the shade. But, even then, I sometimes saw only the passing wave of a white robe; or a lovely arm or neck gleamed by in the moonshine; or white feet went walking alone over the moony sward. Nor, I grieve to say, did I ever come much nearer to these glorious beings, or ever look upon the Queen of the Fairies herself. My destiny ordered otherwise.

In this palace of marble and silver, and fountains and moonshine, I spent many days; waited upon constantly in my room with everything desirable, and bathing daily in the fairy bath. All this time I was little troubled with my demon shadow I had a vague feeling that he was somewhere about the palace; but it seemed as if the hope that I should in this place be finally freed from his hated presence, had sufficed to banish him for a time. How and where I found him, I shall soon have to relate.

The third day after my arrival, I found the library of the palace; and here, all the time I remained, I spent most of the middle of the day. For it was, not to mention far greater attractions, a luxurious retreat from the noontide sun. During the mornings and afternoons, I wandered about the lovely neighbourhood, or lay, lost in delicious day-dreams, beneath some mighty tree on the open lawn. My evenings were by-and-by spent in a part of the palace, the account of which, and of my adventures in connection with it, I must yet postpone for a little.

The library was a mighty hall, lighted from the roof, which was formed of something like glass, vaulted over in a single piece, and stained throughout with a great mysterious picture in gorgeous colouring.

The walls were lined from floor to roof with books and books: most of them in ancient bindings, but some in strange new fashions which I had never seen, and which, were I to make the attempt, I could ill describe. All around the walls, in front of the books, ran galleries in rows, communicating by stairs. These galleries were built of all kinds of coloured stones; all sorts of marble and granite, with porphyry, jasper, lapis lazuli, agate, and various others, were ranged in wonderful melody of successive colours. Although the material, then, of which these galleries and stairs were built, rendered necessary a certain degree of massiveness in the construction, yet such was the size of the place, that they seemed to run along the walls like cords.

Over some parts of the library, descended curtains of silk of various dyes, none of which I ever saw lifted while I was there; and I felt somehow that it would be presumptuous in me to venture to look within them. But the use of the other books seemed free; and day after day I came to the library, threw myself on one of the many sumptuous eastern carpets, which lay here and there on the floor, and read, and read, until weary; if that can be designated as weariness, which was rather the faintness of rapturous delight; or until, sometimes, the failing of the light invited me to go abroad, in the hope that a cool gentle breeze might have arisen to bathe, with an airy invigorating bath, the limbs which the glow of the burning spirit within had withered no less than the glow of the blazing sun without.

One peculiarity of these books, or at least most of those I looked into, I must make a somewhat vain attempt to describe.

If, for instance, it was a book of metaphysics I opened, I had scarcely read two pages before I seemed to myself to be pondering over discovered truth, and constructing the intellectual machine whereby to communicate the discovery to my fellow men. With some books, however, of this nature, it seemed rather as if the process was removed yet a great way further back; and I was trying to find the root of a manifestation, the spiritual truth whence a material vision sprang; or to combine two propositions, both apparently true, either at once or in different remembered moods, and to find the point in which their invisibly converging lines would unite in one, revealing a truth higher than either and differing from both; though so far from being opposed to either, that it was that whence each derived its life and power. Or if the book was one of travels, I found myself the traveller. New lands, fresh experiences, novel customs, rose around me. I walked, I discovered, I fought, I suffered, I rejoiced in my success. Was it a history? I was the chief actor therein. I suffered my own blame; I was glad in my own praise. With a fiction it was the same. Mine was the whole story. For I took the place of the character who was most like myself, and his story was mine; until, grown weary with the life of years condensed in an hour, or arrived at my deathbed, or the end of the volume, I would awake, with a sudden bewilderment, to the consciousness of my present life, recognising the walls and roof around me, and finding I joyed or sorrowed only in a book. If the book was a poem, the words disappeared, or took the subordinate position of an accompaniment to the succession of forms and images that rose and vanished with a soundless rhythm, and a hidden rime.

In one, with a mystical title, which I cannot recall, I read of a world that is not like ours. The wondrous account, in such a feeble, fragmentary way as is possible to me, I would willingly impart. Whether or not it was all a poem, I cannot tell; but, from the impulse I felt, when I first contemplated writing it, to break into rime, to which impulse I shall give way if it comes upon me again, I think it must have been, partly at least, in verse.

CHAPTER XII

"Chained is the Spring. The night-wind bold
Blows over the hard earth;
Time is not more confused and cold,
Nor keeps more wintry mirth.

"Yet blow, and roll the world about;
Blow, Time—blow, winter's Wind!
Through chinks of Time, heaven peepeth out,
And Spring the frost behind."
G. E. M.

They who believe in the influences of the stars over the fates of men, are, in feeling at least, nearer the truth than they who regard the heavenly bodies as related to them merely by a common obedience to an external law. All that man sees has to do with man. Worlds cannot be without an intermundane relationship. The community of the centre of all creation suggests an interradiating connection and dependence of the parts. Else a grander idea is conceivable than that which is already imbodied. The blank, which is only a forgotten life, lying behind the consciousness, and the misty splendour, which is an undeveloped life, lying before it, may be full of mysterious revelations of other connexions with the worlds around us, than those of science and poetry. No shining belt or gleaming moon, no red and green glory in a self-encircling twin-star, but has a relation with the hidden things of a man's soul, and, it may be, with the secret history of his body as well. They are portions of the living house wherein he abides.

Through the realms of the monarch Sun
Creeps a world, whose course had begun,
On a weary path with a weary pace,
Before the Earth sprang forth on her race:
But many a time the Earth had sped
Around the path she still must tread,
Ere the elder planet, on leaden wing,
Once circled the court of the planet's king.

61

There, in that lonely and distant star,
The seasons are not as our seasons are;
But many a year hath Autumn to dress
The trees in their matron loveliness;
As long hath old Winter in triumph to go
O'er beauties dead in his vaults below;
And many a year the Spring doth wear
Combing the icicles from her hair;
And Summer, dear Summer, hath years of June,
With large white clouds, and cool showers at noon:
And a beauty that grows to a weight like grief,
Till a burst of tears is the heart's relief.

Children, born when Winter is king,
May never rejoice in the hoping Spring;
Though their own heart-buds are bursting with joy,
And the child hath grown to the girl or boy;
But may die with cold and icy hours
Watching them ever in place of flowers.
And some who awake from their primal sleep,
When the sighs of Summer through forests creep,
Live, and love, and are loved again;
Seek for pleasure, and find its pain;
Sink to their last, their forsaken sleeping,
With the same sweet odours around them creeping.

Now the children, there, are not born as the children are born in worlds nearer to the sun. For they arrive no one knows how. A maiden, walking alone, hears a cry: for even there a cry is the first utterance; and searching about, she findeth, under an overhanging rock, or within a clump of bushes, or, it may be, betwixt gray stones on the side of a hill, or in any other sheltered and unexpected spot, a little child. This she taketh tenderly, and beareth home with joy, calling out, "Mother, mother"—if so be that her mother lives—"I have got a baby—I have found a child!" All the household gathers round to see;—"*Where is it? What is it like? Where did you find it?*" and such-like questions, abounding. And thereupon she relates the whole story of the discovery; for by the circumstances, such as season of the year, time of the day, condition of the air, and such like, and, especially, the peculiar and never-repeated aspect of the heavens and earth at the time, and the nature of the place of shelter wherein it is found, is determined, or at least indicated, the nature of the child thus discovered. Therefore, at certain seasons, and in certain states of the weather, according, in part, to their own fancy, the young women go out to look for children. They generally avoid seeking them, though they cannot help sometimes finding them, in places and with circumstances uncongenial to their peculiar likings. But no sooner is a child found, than its claim for protection and nurture obliterates all feeling of choice in the matter. Chiefly, however, in the season of summer, which lasts so long, coming as it does after such long intervals; and mostly in the warm evenings, about the middle of twilight; and principally in the woods and along the river banks, do the maidens go looking for children just as children look for flowers. And ever as the child grows, yea, more and more as he advances in years, will his face indicate to those who understand the spirit of Nature, and her utterances in the face of the world, the nature of the place of his birth, and the other circumstances thereof; whether a clear morning sun guided his mother to the nook whence issued the boy's low cry; or at eve the lonely maiden (for the same woman never finds a second, at least while the first lives) discovers the girl by the glimmer of her white skin, lying in a nest like that of the lark, amid long encircling grasses, and the upward-gazing eyes of the lowly daisies; whether the storm bowed the forest trees around, or the still frost fixed in silence the else flowing and babbling stream.

After they grow up, the men and women are but little together. There is this peculiar difference between them, which likewise distinguishes the women from those of the earth. The men alone have arms; the women have only wings. Resplendent wings are they, wherein they can shroud themselves from head to foot in a panoply of glistering glory. By these wings alone, it may frequently be judged in what seasons, and under what aspects, they were born. From those that came in winter, go great white wings, white as snow; the edge of every feather shining like the sheen of silver, so that they flash and glitter like frost in the sun. But underneath, they are tinged with a faint pink or rose-colour. Those born in spring have wings of a brilliant green, green as grass; and towards the edges the feathers are enamelled like the surface of the grass-blades. These again are white within. Those that are born in summer have wings of a deep rose-colour, lined with pale gold. And those born in autumn have purple wings, with a rich brown on the inside. But these colours are modified and altered in all varieties, corresponding to the mood of the day and hour, as well as the season of the year; and sometimes I found the various colours so intermingled, that I could not determine even the season, though doubtless the hieroglyphic could be deciphered by more experienced eyes. One splendour, in particular, I remember—wings of deep carmine, with an inner down of warm gray, around a form of brilliant whiteness.

She had been found as the sun went down through a low sea-fog, casting crimson along a broad sea-path into a little cave on the shore, where a bathing maiden saw her lying.

But though I speak of sun and fog, and sea and shore, the world there is in some respects very different from the earth whereon men live. For instance, the waters reflect no forms. To the unaccustomed eye they appear, if undisturbed, like the surface of a dark metal, only that the latter would reflect indistinctly, whereas they reflect not at all, except light which falls immediately upon them. This has a great effect in causing the landscapes to differ from those on the earth. On the stillest evening, no tall ship on the sea sends a long wavering reflection almost to the feet of him on shore; the face of no maiden brightens at its own beauty in a still forest-well. The sun and moon alone make a glitter on the surface. The sea is like a sea of death, ready to ingulf and never to reveal: a visible shadow of oblivion. Yet the women sport in its waters like gorgeous sea-birds. The men more rarely enter them. But, on the contrary, the sky reflects everything beneath it, as if it were built of water like ours. Of course, from its concavity there is some distortion of the reflected objects; yet wondrous combinations of form are often to be seen in the overhanging depth. And then it is not shaped so much like a round dome as the sky of the earth, but, more of an egg-shape, rises to a great towering height in the middle, appearing far more lofty than the other. When the stars come out at night, it shows a mighty cupola, "fretted with golden fires," wherein there is room for all tempests to rush and rave.

One evening in early summer, I stood with a group of men and women on a steep rock that overhung the sea. They were all questioning me about my world and the ways thereof. In making reply to one of their questions, I was compelled to say that children are not born in the Earth as with them. Upon this I was assailed with a whole battery of inquiries, which at first I tried to avoid; but, at last, I was compelled, in the vaguest manner I could invent, to make some approach to the subject in question. Immediately a dim notion of what I meant, seemed to dawn in the minds of most of the women. Some of them folded their great wings all around them, as they generally do when in the least offended, and stood erect and motionless. One spread out her rosy pinions, and flashed from the promontory into the gulf at its foot. A great light shone in the eyes of one maiden, who turned and walked slowly away, with her purple and white wings half dispread behind her. She was found, the next morning, dead beneath a withered tree on a bare hill-side, some miles inland. They buried her where she lay, as is their custom; for, before they die, they instinctively search for a spot like the place of their birth, and having found one that satisfies them, they lie down, fold their wings around them, if they be women, or cross their arms over their breasts, if they are men, just as if they were going to sleep; and so sleep indeed. The sign or cause of coming death is an indescribable longing for something, they know not what, which seizes them, and drives them into solitude, consuming them within, till the body fails. When a youth and a maiden look too deep into each other's eyes, this longing seizes and possesses them; but instead of drawing nearer to each other, they wander away, each alone, into solitary places, and die of their desire. But it seems to me, that thereafter they are born babes upon our earth: where, if, when grown, they find each other, it goes well with them; if not, it will seem to go ill. But of this I know nothing. When I told them that the women on the Earth had not wings like them, but arms, they stared, and said how bold and masculine they must look; not knowing that their wings, glorious as they are, are but undeveloped arms.

But see the power of this book, that, while recounting what I can recall of its contents, I write as if myself had visited the far-off planet, learned its ways and appearances, and conversed with its men and women. And so, while writing, it seemed to me that I had.

The book goes on with the story of a maiden, who, born at the close of autumn, and living in a long, to her endless winter, set out at last to find the regions of spring; for, as in our earth, the seasons are divided over the globe. It begins something like this:

> She watched them dying for many a day,
> Dropping from off the old trees away,
> One by one; or else in a shower
> Crowding over the withered flower
> For as if they had done some grievous wrong,
> The sun, that had nursed them and loved them so long,
> Grew weary of loving, and, turning back,
> Hastened away on his southern track;
> And helplessly hung each shrivelled leaf,
> Faded away with an idle grief.
> And the gusts of wind, sad Autumn's sighs,
> Mournfully swept through their families;
> Casting away with a helpless moan
> All that he yet might call his own,
> As the child, when his bird is gone for ever,
> Flingeth the cage on the wandering river.
> And the giant trees, as bare as Death,
> Slowly bowed to the great Wind's breath;

And groaned with trying to keep from groaning
Amidst the young trees bending and moaning.
And the ancient planet's mighty sea
Was heaving and falling most restlessly,
And the tops of the waves were broken and white,
Tossing about to ease their might;
And the river was striving to reach the main,
And the ripple was hurrying back again.
Nature lived in sadness now;
Sadness lived on the maiden's brow,
As she watched, with a fixed, half-conscious eye,
One lonely leaf that trembled on high,
Till it dropped at last from the desolate bough—
Sorrow, oh, sorrow! 'tis winter now.
And her tears gushed forth, though it was but a leaf,
For little will loose the swollen fountain of grief:
When up to the lip the water goes,
It needs but a drop, and it overflows.

Oh! many and many a dreary year
Must pass away ere the buds appear:
Many a night of darksome sorrow
Yield to the light of a joyless morrow,
Ere birds again, on the clothed trees,
Shall fill the branches with melodies.
She will dream of meadows with wakeful streams;
Of wavy grass in the sunny beams;
Of hidden wells that soundless spring,
Hoarding their joy as a holy thing;
Of founts that tell it all day long
To the listening woods, with exultant song;
She will dream of evenings that die into nights,
Where each sense is filled with its own delights,
And the soul is still as the vaulted sky,
Lulled with an inner harmony;

And the flowers give out to the dewy night,
Changed into perfume, the gathered light;
And the darkness sinks upon all their host,
Till the sun sail up on the eastern coast—
She will wake and see the branches bare,
Weaving a net in the frozen air.

The story goes on to tell how, at last, weary with wintriness, she travelled towards the southern regions of her globe, to meet the spring on its slow way northwards; and how, after many sad adventures, many disappointed hopes, and many tears, bitter and fruitless, she found at last, one stormy afternoon, in a leafless forest, a single snowdrop growing betwixt the borders of the winter and spring. She lay down beside it and died. I almost believe that a child, pale and peaceful as a snowdrop, was born in the Earth within a fixed season from that stormy afternoon.

CHAPTER XIII

"I saw a ship sailing upon the sea
Deeply laden as ship could be;
But not so deep as in love I am
For I care not whether I sink or swim."
Old Ballad.

"But Love is such a Mystery
I cannot find it out:
For when I think I'm best resolv'd,
I then am in most doubt."
SIR JOHN SUCKLING.

One story I will try to reproduce. But, alas! it is like trying to reconstruct a forest out of broken branches and withered leaves. In the fairy book, everything was just as it should be, though whether in words or something else, I cannot tell. It glowed and flashed the thoughts upon the soul, with such a power that the medium disappeared from the consciousness, and it was occupied only with the things themselves. My representation of it must resemble a translation from a rich and powerful language, capable of embodying the thoughts of a splendidly developed people, into the meagre and half-articulate speech of a savage tribe. Of course, while I read it, I was Cosmo, and his history was mine. Yet, all the time, I seemed to have a kind of double consciousness, and the story a double meaning. Sometimes it seemed only to represent a simple story of ordinary life, perhaps almost of universal life; wherein two souls, loving each other and longing to come nearer, do, after all, but behold each other as in a glass darkly.
As through the hard rock go the branching silver veins; as into the solid

land run the creeks and gulfs from the unresting sea; as the lights and influences of the upper worlds sink silently through the earth's atmosphere; so doth Faerie invade the world of men, and sometimes startle the common eye with an association as of cause and effect, when between the two no connecting links can be traced.

Cosmo von Wehrstahl was a student at the University of Prague. Though of a noble family, he was poor, and prided himself upon the independence that poverty gives; for what will not a man pride himself upon, when he cannot get rid of it? A favourite with his fellow students, he yet had no companions; and none of them had ever crossed the threshold of his lodging in the top of one of the highest houses in the old town. Indeed, the secret of much of that complaisance which recommended him to his fellows, was the thought of his unknown retreat, whither in the evening he could betake himself and indulge undisturbed in his own studies and reveries. These studies, besides those subjects necessary to his course at the University, embraced some less commonly known and approved; for in a secret drawer lay the works of Albertus Magnus and Cornelius Agrippa, along with others less read and more abstruse. As yet, however, he had followed these researches only from curiosity, and had turned them to no practical purpose.

His lodging consisted of one large low-ceiled room, singularly bare of furniture; for besides a couple of wooden chairs, a couch which served for dreaming on both by day and night, and a great press of black oak, there was very little in the room that could be called furniture.

But curious instruments were heaped in the corners; and in one stood a skeleton, half-leaning against the wall, half-supported by a string about its neck. One of its hands, all of fingers, rested on the heavy pommel of a great sword that stood beside it.

Various weapons were scattered about over the floor. The walls were utterly bare of adornment; for the few strange things, such as a large dried bat with wings dispread, the skin of a porcupine, and a stuffed sea-mouse, could hardly be reckoned as such. But although his fancy delighted in vagaries like these, he indulged his imagination with far different fare. His mind had never yet been filled with an absorbing passion; but it lay like a still twilight open to any wind, whether the low breath that wafts but odours, or the storm that bows the great trees till they strain and creak. He saw everything as through a rose-coloured glass. When he looked from his window on the street below, not a maiden passed but she moved as in a story, and drew his thoughts after her till she disappeared in the vista. When he walked in the streets, he always felt as if reading a tale, into which he sought to weave every face of interest that went by; and every sweet voice swept his soul as with the wing of a passing angel. He was in fact a poet without words; the more absorbed and endangered, that the springing-waters were dammed back into his soul, where, finding no utterance, they grew, and swelled, and undermined. He used to lie on his hard couch, and read a tale or a poem, till the book dropped from his hand; but he dreamed on, he knew not whether awake or asleep, until the opposite roof grew upon his sense, and turned golden in the sunrise. Then he arose too; and the impulses of vigorous youth kept him ever active, either in study or in sport, until again the close of the day left him free; and the world of night, which had lain drowned in the cataract of the day, rose up in his soul, with all its stars, and dim-seen phantom shapes. But this could hardly last long. Some one form must sooner or later step within the charmed circle, enter the house of life, and compel the bewildered magician to kneel and worship.

One afternoon, towards dusk, he was wandering dreamily in one of the principal streets, when a fellow student roused him by a slap on the shoulder, and asked him to accompany him into a little back alley to look at some old armour which he had taken a fancy to possess. Cosmo was considered an authority in every matter pertaining to arms, ancient or modern. In the use of weapons, none of the students could come near him; and his practical acquaintance with some had principally contributed to establish his authority in reference to all. He accompanied him willingly.

They entered a narrow alley, and thence a dirty little court, where a low arched door admitted them into a heterogeneous assemblage of everything musty, and dusty, and old, that could well be imagined. His verdict on the armour was satisfactory, and his companion at once concluded the purchase. As they were leaving the place, Cosmo's eye was attracted by an old mirror of an elliptical shape, which leaned against the wall, covered with dust. Around it was some curious carving, which he could see but very indistinctly by the glimmering light which the owner of the shop carried in his hand. It was this carving that attracted his attention; at least so it appeared to him. He left the place, however, with his friend, taking no further notice of it. They walked together to the main street, where they parted and took opposite directions.

No sooner was Cosmo left alone, than the thought of the curious old mirror returned to him. A strong desire to see it more plainly arose within him, and he directed his steps once more towards the shop. The owner opened the door when he knocked, as if he had expected him. He was a little, old, withered man, with a hooked nose, and burning eyes constantly in a slow restless motion, and looking here and there as if after something that eluded them. Pretending to examine several other articles, Cosmo at last approached the mirror, and requested to have it taken down.

"Take it down yourself, master; I cannot reach it," said the old man.

Cosmo took it down carefully, when he saw that the carving was indeed delicate and costly, being both of admirable design and execution; containing withal many devices which seemed to embody some meaning to which he had no clue. This, naturally, in one of his tastes and temperament, increased the interest he felt in the old mirror; so much, indeed, that he now longed to possess it, in order to study its frame at his leisure. He pretended, however, to want it only for use; and saying he feared the plate could be of little service, as it was rather old, he brushed away a little of the dust from its face, expecting to see a dull reflection within. His surprise was great when he found the reflection brilliant, revealing a glass not only uninjured by age, but wondrously clear and perfect (should the whole correspond to this part) even for one newly from the hands of the maker. He asked carelessly what the owner wanted for the thing. The old man replied by mentioning a sum of money far beyond the reach of poor Cosmo, who proceeded to replace the mirror where it had stood before.

"You think the price too high?" said the old man.

"I do not know that it is too much for you to ask," replied Cosmo; "but it is far too much for me to give."

The old man held up his light towards Cosmo's face. "I like your look," said he.

Cosmo could not return the compliment. In fact, now he looked closely at him for the first time, he felt a kind of repugnance to him, mingled with a strange feeling of doubt whether a man or a woman stood before him.

"What is your name?" he continued.

"Cosmo von Wehrstahl."

"Ah, ah! I thought as much. I see your father in you. I knew your father very well, young sir. I dare say in some odd corners of my house, you might find some old things with his crest and cipher upon them still. Well, I like you: you shall have the mirror at the fourth part of what I asked for it; but upon one condition."

"What is that?" said Cosmo; for, although the price was still a great deal for him to give, he could just manage it; and the desire to possess the mirror had increased to an altogether unaccountable degree, since it had seemed beyond his reach.

"That if you should ever want to get rid of it again, you will let me have the first offer."

"Certainly," replied Cosmo, with a smile; adding, "a moderate condition indeed."

"On your honour?" insisted the seller.

"On my honour," said the buyer; and the bargain was concluded.

"I will carry it home for you," said the old man, as Cosmo took it in his hands.

"No, no; I will carry it myself," said he; for he had a peculiar dislike to revealing his residence to any one, and more especially to this person, to whom he felt every moment a greater antipathy. "Just as you please," said the old creature, and muttered to himself as he held his light at the door to show him out of the court: "Sold for the sixth time! I wonder what will be the upshot of it this time. I should think my lady had enough of it by now!"

Cosmo carried his prize carefully home. But all the way he had an uncomfortable feeling that he was watched and dogged. Repeatedly he looked about, but saw nothing to justify his suspicions. Indeed, the streets were too crowded and too ill lighted to expose very readily a careful spy, if such there should be at his heels. He reached his lodging in safety, and leaned his purchase against the wall, rather relieved, strong as he was, to be rid of its weight; then, lighting his pipe, threw himself on the couch, and was soon lapt in the folds of one of his haunting dreams.

He returned home earlier than usual the next day, and fixed the mirror to the wall, over the hearth, at one end of his long room.

He then carefully wiped away the dust from its face, and, clear as the water of a sunny spring, the mirror shone out from beneath the envious covering. But his interest was chiefly occupied with the curious carving of the frame. This he cleaned as well as he could with a brush; and then he proceeded to a minute examination of its various parts, in the hope of discovering some index to the intention of the carver. In this, however, he was unsuccessful; and, at length, pausing with some weariness and disappointment, he gazed vacantly for a few moments into the depth of the reflected room. But ere long he said, half aloud: "What a strange thing a mirror is! and what a wondrous affinity exists between it and a man's imagination! For this room of mine, as I behold it in the glass, is the same, and yet not the same. It is not the mere representation of the room I live in, but it looks just as if I were reading about it in a story I like. All its commonness has disappeared. The mirror has lifted it out of the region of fact into the realm of art; and the very representing of it to me has clothed with interest that which was otherwise hard and bare; just as one sees with delight upon the stage the representation of a character from which one would escape in life as from something unendurably wearisome. But is it not rather that art rescues nature from the weary and sated regards of our senses, and the degrading injustice of our anxious everyday life, and, appealing to the imagination, which dwells apart, reveals Nature in some degree as she really is, and as she represents herself to the eye of the child, whose every-day life, fearless and unambitious, meets the true import of the wonder-teeming world around him, and rejoices therein without questioning? That skeleton, now—I almost fear it, standing there so still, with eyes only for the unseen, like a watch-tower looking across all the waste of this busy world into the quiet regions of rest beyond. And yet I know every bone and every joint in it as well as my own fist. And that old battle-axe looks as if any moment it might be caught up by a mailed hand, and, borne forth by the mighty arm, go crashing through casque, and skull, and brain, invading the Unknown with yet another bewildered ghost. I should like to live in *that* room if I could only get into it."

Scarcely had the half-moulded words floated from him, as he stood gazing into the mirror, when, striking him as with a flash of amazement that fixed him in his posture, noiseless and unannounced, glided suddenly through the door into the reflected room, with stately motion, yet reluctant and faltering step, the graceful form of a woman, clothed all in white. Her back only was visible as she walked slowly up to the couch in the further end of the room, on which she laid herself wearily, turning towards him a face of unutterable loveliness, in which suffering, and dislike, and a sense of compulsion, strangely mingled with the beauty. He stood without the power of motion for some moments, with his eyes irrecoverably fixed upon her; and even after he was conscious of the ability to move, he could not summon up courage to turn and look on her, face to face, in the veritable chamber in which he stood. At length, with a sudden effort, in which the exercise of the will was so pure, that it seemed involuntary, he turned his face to the couch. It was vacant. In bewilderment, mingled with terror, he turned again to the mirror: there, on the reflected couch, lay the exquisite lady-form. She lay with closed eyes, whence two large tears were just welling from beneath the veiling lids; still as death, save for the convulsive motion of her bosom.

Cosmo himself could not have described what he felt. His emotions were of a kind that destroyed consciousness, and could never be clearly recalled. He could not help standing yet by the mirror, and keeping his eyes fixed on the lady, though he was painfully aware of his rudeness, and feared every moment that she would open hers, and meet his fixed regard. But he was, ere long, a little relieved; for, after a while, her eyelids slowly rose, and her eyes remained uncovered, but unemployed for a time; and when, at length, they began to wander about the room, as if languidly seeking to make some acquaintance with her environment, they were never directed towards him: it seemed nothing but what was in the mirror could affect her vision; and, therefore, if she saw him at all, it could only be his back, which, of necessity, was turned towards her in the glass. The two figures in the mirror could not meet face to face, except he turned and looked at her, present in his room; and, as she was not there, he concluded that if he were to turn towards the part in his room corresponding to that in which she lay, his reflection would either be invisible to her altogether, or at least it must appear to her to gaze vacantly towards her, and no meeting of the eyes would produce the impression of spiritual proximity. By-and-by her eyes fell upon the skeleton, and he saw her shudder and close them. She did not open them again, but signs of repugnance continued evident on her countenance. Cosmo would have removed the obnoxious thing at once, but he feared to discompose her yet more by the assertion of his presence which the act would involve. So he stood and watched her. The eyelids yet shrouded the eyes, as a costly case the jewels within; the troubled expression gradually faded from the countenance, leaving only a faint sorrow behind; the features settled into an unchanging expression of rest; and by these signs, and the slow regular motion of her breathing, Cosmo knew that she slept. He could now gaze on her without embarrassment. He saw that her figure, dressed in the simplest robe of white, was worthy of her face; and so harmonious, that either the delicately moulded foot, or any finger of the equally delicate hand, was an index to the whole. As she lay, her whole form manifested the relaxation of perfect repose. He gazed till he was weary, and at last seated himself near the new-found shrine, and mechanically took up a book, like one who watches by a sick-bed. But his eyes gathered no thoughts from the page before him. His intellect had been stunned by the bold contradiction, to its face, of all its experience, and now lay passive, without assertion, or speculation, or even conscious astonishment; while his imagination sent one wild dream of blessedness after another coursing through his soul. How long he sat he knew not; but at length he roused himself, rose, and, trembling in every portion of his frame, looked again into the mirror. She was gone. The mirror reflected faithfully what his room presented, and nothing more. It stood there like a golden setting whence the central jewel has been stolen away—like a night-sky without the glory of its stars. She had carried with her all the strangeness of the reflected room. It had sunk to the level of the one without.

But when the first pangs of his disappointment had passed, Cosmo began to comfort himself with the hope that she might return, perhaps the next evening, at the same hour. Resolving that if she did, she should not at least be scared by the hateful skeleton, he removed that and several other articles of questionable appearance into a recess by the side of the hearth, whence they could not possibly cast any reflection into the mirror; and having made his poor room as tidy as he could, sought the solace of the open sky and of a night wind that had begun to blow, for he could not rest where he was. When he returned, somewhat composed, he could hardly prevail with himself to lie down on his bed; for he could not help feeling as if she had lain upon it; and for him to lie there now would be something like sacrilege. However, weariness prevailed; and laying himself on the couch, dressed as he was, he slept till day.

With a beating heart, beating till he could hardly breathe, he stood in dumb hope before the mirror, on the following evening. Again the reflected room shone as through a purple vapour in the gathering twilight. Everything seemed waiting like himself for a coming splendour to glorify its poor earthliness with the presence of a heavenly joy. And just as the room vibrated with the strokes of the neighbouring church bell, announcing the hour of six, in glided the pale beauty, and again laid herself on the couch. Poor Cosmo nearly lost his senses with delight. She was there once more! Her eyes sought the corner where the skeleton had stood, and a faint gleam of satisfaction crossed her face, apparently at seeing it empty. She looked suffering still, but there was less of discomfort expressed in her countenance than there had been the night before. She took more notice of the things about her, and seemed to gaze with some curiosity on the strange apparatus standing here and there in her room. At length, however, drowsiness seemed to overtake her, and again she fell asleep. Resolved not to lose sight of her this time, Cosmo watched the sleeping form. Her slumber was so deep and absorbing that a fascinating repose seemed to pass contagiously from her to him as he gazed upon her; and he started as if from a dream, when the lady moved, and, without opening her eyes, rose, and passed from the room with the gait of a somnambulist.

Cosmo was now in a state of extravagant delight. Most men have a secret treasure somewhere. The miser has his golden hoard; the virtuoso his pet ring; the student his rare book; the poet his favourite haunt; the lover his secret drawer; but Cosmo had a mirror with a lovely lady in it. And now that he knew by the skeleton, that she was affected by the things around her, he had a new object in life: he would turn the bare chamber in the mirror into a room such as no lady need disdain to call her own. This he could effect only by furnishing and adorning his. And Cosmo was poor. Yet he possessed accomplishments that could be turned to account; although, hitherto, he had preferred living on his slender allowance, to increasing his means by what his pride considered unworthy of his rank. He was the best swordsman in the University; and now he offered to give lessons in fencing and similar exercises, to such as chose to pay him well for the trouble. His proposal was heard with surprise by the students; but it was eagerly accepted by many; and soon his instructions were not confined to the richer students, but were anxiously sought by many of the young nobility of Prague and its neighbourhood. So that very soon he had a good deal of money at his command. The first thing he did was to remove his apparatus and oddities into a closet in the room. Then he placed his bed and a few other necessaries on each side of the hearth, and parted them from the rest of the room by two screens of Indian fabric. Then he put an elegant couch for the lady to lie upon, in the corner where his bed had formerly stood; and, by degrees, every day adding some article of luxury, converted it, at length, into a rich boudoir.

Every night, about the same time, the lady entered. The first time she saw the new couch, she started with a half-smile; then her face grew very sad, the tears came to her eyes, and she laid herself upon the couch, and pressed her face into the silken cushions, as if to hide from everything. She took notice of each addition and each change as the work proceeded; and a look of acknowledgment, as if she knew that some one was ministering to her, and was grateful for it, mingled with the constant look of suffering. At length, after she had lain down as usual one evening, her eyes fell upon some paintings with which Cosmo had just finished adorning the walls. She rose, and to his great delight, walked across the room, and proceeded to examine them carefully, testifying much pleasure in her looks as she did so. But again the sorrowful, tearful expression returned, and again she buried her face in the pillows of her couch. Gradually, however, her countenance had grown more composed; much of the suffering manifest on her first appearance had vanished, and a kind of quiet, hopeful expression had taken its place; which, however, frequently gave way to an anxious, troubled look, mingled with something of sympathetic pity.

Meantime, how fared Cosmo? As might be expected in one of his temperament, his interest had blossomed into love, and his love—shall I call it *ripened*, or—*withered* into passion. But, alas! he loved a shadow. He could not come near her, could not speak to her, could not hear a sound from those sweet lips, to which his longing eyes would cling like bees to their honey-founts. Ever and anon he sang to himself:

"I shall die for love of the maiden;"

and ever he looked again, and died not, though his heart seemed ready to break with intensity of life and longing. And the more he did for her, the more he loved her; and he hoped that, although she never appeared to see him, yet she was pleased to think that one unknown would give his life to her. He tried to comfort himself over his separation from her, by thinking that perhaps some day she would see him and make signs to him, and that would satisfy him; "for," thought he, "is not this all that a loving soul can do to enter into communion with another? Nay, how many who love never come nearer than to behold each other as in a mirror; seem to know and yet never know the inward life; never enter the other soul; and part at last, with but the vaguest notion of the universe on the borders of which they have been hovering for years? If I could but speak to her, and knew that she heard me, I should be satisfied." Once he contemplated painting a picture on the wall, which should, of necessity, convey to the lady a thought of himself; but, though he had some skill with the pencil, he found his hand tremble so much when he began the attempt, that he was forced to give it up. . . . . .

"Who lives, he dies; who dies, he is alive."

One evening, as he stood gazing on his treasure, he thought he saw a faint expression of self-consciousness on her countenance, as if she surmised that passionate eyes were fixed upon her. This grew; till at last the red blood rose over her neck, and cheek, and brow. Cosmo's longing to approach her became almost delirious. This night she was dressed in an evening costume, resplendent with diamonds. This could add nothing to her beauty, but it presented it in a new aspect; enabled her loveliness to make a new manifestation of itself in a new embodiment. For essential beauty is infinite; and, as the soul of Nature needs an endless succession of varied forms to embody her loveliness, countless faces of beauty springing forth, not any two the same, at any one of her heart-throbs; so the individual form needs an infinite change of its environments, to enable it to uncover all the phases of its loveliness. Diamonds glittered from amidst her hair, half hidden in its luxuriance, like stars through dark rain-clouds; and the bracelets on her white arms flashed all the colours of a rainbow of lightnings, as she lifted her snowy hands to cover her burning face. But her beauty shone down all its adornment. "If I might have but one of her feet to kiss," thought Cosmo, "I should be content." Alas! he deceived himself, for passion is never content. Nor did he know that there are *two* ways out of her enchanted house. But, suddenly, as if the pang had been driven into his heart from without, revealing itself first in pain, and afterwards in definite form, the thought darted into his mind, "She has a lover somewhere. Remembered words of his bring the colour on her face now. I am nowhere to her. She lives in another world all day, and all night, after she leaves me. Why does she come and make me love her, till I, a strong man, am too faint to look upon her more?" He looked again, and her face was pale as a lily. A sorrowful compassion seemed to rebuke the glitter of the restless jewels, and the slow tears rose in her eyes. She left her room sooner this evening than was her wont. Cosmo remained alone, with a feeling as if his bosom had been suddenly left empty and hollow, and the weight of the whole world was crushing in its walls. The next evening, for the first time since she began to come, she came not.

And now Cosmo was in wretched plight. Since the thought of a rival had occurred to him, he could not rest for a moment. More than ever he longed to see the lady face to face. He persuaded himself that if he but knew the worst he would be satisfied; for then he could abandon Prague, and find that relief in constant motion, which is the hope of all active minds when invaded by distress. Meantime he waited with unspeakable anxiety for the next night, hoping she would return: but she did not appear. And now he fell really ill. Rallied by his fellow students on his wretched looks, he ceased to attend the lectures. His engagements were neglected. He cared for nothing. The sky, with the great sun in it, was to him a heartless, burning desert. The men and women in the streets were mere puppets, without motives in themselves, or interest to him. He saw them all as on the ever-changing field of a *camera obscura*. She—she alone and altogether—was his universe, his well of life, his incarnate good. For six evenings she came not. Let his absorbing passion, and the slow fever that was consuming his brain, be his excuse for the resolution which he had taken and begun to execute, before that time had expired.

Reasoning with himself, that it must be by some enchantment connected with the mirror, that the form of the lady was to be seen in it, he determined to attempt to turn to account what he had hitherto studied principally from curiosity. "For," said he to himself, "if a spell can force her presence in that glass (and she came unwillingly at first), may not a stronger spell, such as I know, especially with the aid of her half-presence in the mirror, if ever she appears again, compel her living form to come to me here? If I do her wrong, let love be my excuse. I want only to know my doom from her own lips." He never doubted, all the time, that she was a real earthly woman; or, rather, that there was a woman, who, somehow or other, threw this reflection of her form into the magic mirror.

He opened his secret drawer, took out his books of magic, lighted his lamp, and read and made notes from midnight till three in the morning, for three successive nights. Then he replaced his books; and the next night went out in quest of the materials necessary for the conjuration. These were not easy to find; for, in love-charms and all incantations of this nature, ingredients are employed scarcely fit to be mentioned, and for the thought even of which, in connexion with her, he could only excuse himself on the score of his bitter need. At length he succeeded in procuring all he required; and on the seventh evening from that on which she had last appeared, he found himself prepared for the exercise of unlawful and tyrannical power.

He cleared the centre of the room; stooped and drew a circle of red on the floor, around the spot where he stood; wrote in the four quarters mystical signs, and numbers which were all powers of seven or nine; examined the whole ring carefully, to see that no smallest break had occurred in the circumference; and then rose from his bending posture. As he rose, the church clock struck seven; and, just as she had appeared the first time, reluctant, slow, and stately, glided in the lady. Cosmo trembled; and when, turning, she revealed a countenance worn and wan, as with sickness or inward trouble, he grew faint, and felt as if he dared not proceed. But as he gazed on the face and form, which now possessed his whole soul, to the exclusion of all other joys and griefs, the longing to speak to her, to know that she heard him, to hear from her one word in return, became so unendurable, that he suddenly and hastily resumed his preparations. Stepping carefully from the circle, he put a small brazier into its centre. He then set fire to its contents of charcoal, and while it burned up, opened his window and seated himself, waiting, beside it.

It was a sultry evening. The air was full of thunder. A sense of luxurious depression filled the brain. The sky seemed to have grown heavy, and to compress the air beneath it. A kind of purplish tinge pervaded the atmosphere, and through the open window came the scents of the distant fields, which all the vapours of the city could not quench. Soon the charcoal glowed. Cosmo sprinkled upon it the incense and other substances which he had compounded, and, stepping within the circle, turned his face from the brazier and towards the mirror. Then, fixing his eyes upon the face of the lady, he began with a trembling voice to repeat a powerful incantation. He had not gone far, before the lady grew pale; and then, like a returning wave, the blood washed all its banks with its crimson tide, and she hid her face in her hands. Then he passed to a conjuration stronger yet.

The lady rose and walked uneasily to and fro in her room. Another spell; and she seemed seeking with her eyes for some object on which they wished to rest. At length it seemed as if she suddenly espied him; for her eyes fixed themselves full and wide upon his, and she drew gradually, and somewhat unwillingly, close to her side of the mirror, just as if his eyes had fascinated her. Cosmo had never seen her so near before. Now at least, eyes met eyes; but he could not quite understand the expression of hers. They were full of tender entreaty, but there was something more that he could not interpret. Though his heart seemed to labour in his throat, he would allow no delight or agitation to turn him from his task. Looking still in her face, he passed on to the mightiest charm he knew. Suddenly the lady turned and walked out of the door of her reflected chamber. A moment after she entered his room with veritable presence; and, forgetting all his precautions, he sprang from the charmed circle, and knelt before her. There she stood, the living lady of his passionate visions, alone beside him, in a thundery twilight, and the glow of a magic fire.

"Why," said the lady, with a trembling voice, "didst thou bring a poor maiden through the rainy streets alone?"

"Because I am dying for love of thee; but I only brought thee from the mirror there."

"Ah, the mirror!" and she looked up at it, and shuddered. "Alas! I am but a slave, while that mirror exists. But do not think it was the power of thy spells that drew me; it was thy longing desire to see me, that beat at the door of my heart, till I was forced to yield."

"Canst thou love me then?" said Cosmo, in a voice calm as death, but almost inarticulate with emotion.

"I do not know," she replied sadly; "that I cannot tell, so long as I am bewildered with enchantments. It were indeed a joy too great, to lay my head on thy bosom and weep to death; for I think thou lovest me, though I do not know;—but——"

Cosmo rose from his knees.

"I love thee as—nay, I know not what—for since I have loved thee, there is nothing else."

He seized her hand: she withdrew it.

"No, better not; I am in thy power, and therefore I may not."

She burst into tears, and kneeling before him in her turn, said—

"Cosmo, if thou lovest me, set me free, even from thyself; break the mirror."

"And shall I see thyself instead?"

"That I cannot tell, I will not deceive thee; we may never meet again."

A fierce struggle arose in Cosmo's bosom. Now she was in his power. She did not dislike him at least; and he could see her when he would. To break the mirror would be to destroy his very life to banish out of his universe the only glory it possessed. The whole world would be but a prison, if he annihilated the one window that looked into the paradise of love. Not yet pure in love, he hesitated.

With a wail of sorrow the lady rose to her feet. "Ah! he loves me not; he loves me not even as I love him; and alas! I care more for his love than even for the freedom I ask."

"I will not wait to be willing," cried Cosmo; and sprang to the corner where the great sword stood.

Meantime it had grown very dark; only the embers cast a red glow through the room. He seized the sword by the steel scabbard, and stood before the mirror; but as he heaved a great blow at it with the heavy pommel, the blade slipped half-way out of the scabbard, and the pommel struck the wall above the mirror. At that moment, a terrible clap of thunder seemed to burst in the very room beside them; and ere Cosmo could repeat the blow, he fell senseless on the hearth. When he came to himself, he found that the lady and the mirror had both disappeared. He was seized with a brain fever, which kept him to his couch for weeks.

When he recovered his reason, he began to think what could have become of the mirror. For the lady, he hoped she had found her way back as she came; but as the mirror involved her fate with its own, he was more immediately anxious about that. He could not think she had carried it away. It was much too heavy, even if it had not been too firmly fixed in the wall, for her to remove it. Then again, he remembered the thunder; which made him believe that it was not the lightning, but some other blow that had struck him down. He concluded that, either by supernatural agency, he having exposed himself to the vengeance of the demons in leaving the circle of safety, or in some other mode, the mirror had probably found its way back to its former owner; and, horrible to think of, might have been by this time once more disposed of, delivering up the lady into the power of another man; who, if he used his power no worse than he himself had done, might yet give Cosmo abundant cause to curse the selfish indecision which prevented him from shattering the mirror at once. Indeed, to think that she whom he loved, and who had prayed to him for freedom, should be still at the mercy, in some degree, of the possessor of the mirror, and was at least exposed to his constant observation, was in itself enough to madden a chary lover.

Anxiety to be well retarded his recovery; but at length he was able to creep abroad. He first made his way to the old broker's, pretending to be in search of something else. A laughing sneer on the creature's face convinced him that he knew all about it; but he could not see it amongst his furniture, or get any information out of him as to what had become of it. He expressed the utmost surprise at hearing it had been stolen, a surprise which Cosmo saw at once to be counterfeited; while, at the same time, he fancied that the old wretch was not at all anxious to have it mistaken for genuine. Full of distress, which he concealed as well as he could, he made many searches, but with no avail. Of course he could ask no questions; but he kept his ears awake for any remotest hint that might set him in a direction of search. He never went out without a short heavy hammer of steel about him, that he might shatter the mirror the moment he was made happy by the sight of his lost treasure, if ever that blessed moment should arrive. Whether he should see the lady again, was now a thought altogether secondary, and postponed to the achievement of her freedom. He wandered here and there, like an anxious ghost, pale and haggard; gnawed ever at the heart, by the thought of what she might be suffering—all from his fault.

One night, he mingled with a crowd that filled the rooms of one of the most distinguished mansions in the city; for he accepted every invitation, that he might lose no chance, however poor, of obtaining some information that might expedite his discovery. Here he wandered about, listening to every stray word that he could catch, in the hope of a revelation. As he approached some ladies who were talking quietly in a corner, one said to another:

"Have you heard of the strange illness of the Princess von Hohenweiss?"

"Yes; she has been ill for more than a year now. It is very sad for so fine a creature to have such a terrible malady. She was better for some weeks lately, but within the last few days the same attacks have returned, apparently accompanied with more suffering than ever. It is altogether an inexplicable story."

"Is there a story connected with her illness?"

"I have only heard imperfect reports of it; but it is said that she gave offence some eighteen months ago to an old woman who had held an office of trust in the family, and who, after some incoherent threats, disappeared. This peculiar affection followed soon after. But the strangest part of the story is its association with the loss of an antique mirror, which stood in her dressing-room, and of which she constantly made use."

Here the speaker's voice sank to a whisper; and Cosmo, although his very soul sat listening in his ears, could hear no more. He trembled too much to dare to address the ladies, even if it had been advisable to expose himself to their curiosity. The name of the Princess was well known to him, but he had never seen her; except indeed it was she, which now he hardly doubted, who had knelt before him on that dreadful night. Fearful of attracting attention, for, from the weak state of his health, he could not recover an appearance of calmness, he made his way to the open air, and reached his lodgings; glad in this, that he at least knew where she lived, although he never dreamed of approaching her openly, even if he should be happy enough to free her from her hateful bondage. He hoped, too, that as he had unexpectedly learned so much, the other and far more important part might be revealed to him ere long.

"Have you seen Steinwald lately?"

"No, I have not seen him for some time. He is almost a match for me at the rapier, and I suppose he thinks he needs no more lessons."

"I wonder what has become of him. I want to see him very much. Let me see; the last time I saw him he was coming out of that old broker's den, to which, if you remember, you accompanied me once, to look at some armour. That is fully three weeks ago."

This hint was enough for Cosmo. Von Steinwald was a man of influence in the court, well known for his reckless habits and fierce passions. The very possibility that the mirror should be in his possession was hell itself to Cosmo. But violent or hasty measures of any sort were most unlikely to succeed. All that he wanted was an opportunity of breaking the fatal glass; and to obtain this he must bide his time. He revolved many plans in his mind, but without being able to fix upon any.

At length, one evening, as he was passing the house of Von Steinwald, he saw the windows more than usually brilliant. He watched for a while, and seeing that company began to arrive, hastened home, and dressed as richly as he could, in the hope of mingling with the guests unquestioned: in effecting which, there could be no difficulty for a man of his carriage.

In a lofty, silent chamber, in another part of the city, lay a form more like marble than a living woman. The loveliness of death seemed frozen upon her face, for her lips were rigid, and her eyelids closed. Her long white hands were crossed over her breast, and no breathing disturbed their repose. Beside the dead, men speak in whispers, as if the deepest rest of all could be broken by the sound of a living voice. Just so, though the soul was evidently beyond the reach of all intimations from the senses, the two ladies, who sat beside her, spoke in the gentlest tones of subdued sorrow. "She has lain so for an hour."

"This cannot last long, I fear."

"How much thinner she has grown within the last few weeks! If she would only speak, and explain what she suffers, it would be better for her. I think she has visions in her trances, but nothing can induce her to refer to them when she is awake."

"Does she ever speak in these trances?"

"I have never heard her; but they say she walks sometimes, and once put the whole household in a terrible fright by disappearing for a whole hour, and returning drenched with rain, and almost dead with exhaustion and fright. But even then she would give no account of what had happened."

A scarce audible murmur from the yet motionless lips of the lady here startled her attendants. After several ineffectual attempts at articulation, the word "*Cosmo!*" burst from her. Then she lay still as before; but only for a moment. With a wild cry, she sprang from the couch erect on the floor, flung her arms above her head, with clasped and straining hands, and, her wide eyes flashing with light, called aloud, with a voice exultant as that of a spirit bursting from a sepulchre, "I am free! I am free! I thank thee!" Then she flung herself on the couch, and sobbed; then rose, and paced wildly up and down the room, with gestures of mingled delight and anxiety. Then turning to her motionless attendants—"Quick, Lisa, my cloak and hood!" Then lower—"I must go to him. Make haste, Lisa! You may come with me, if you will."

In another moment they were in the street, hurrying along towards one of the bridges over the Moldau. The moon was near the zenith, and the streets were almost empty. The Princess soon outstripped her attendant, and was half-way over the bridge, before the other reached it.

"Are you free, lady? The mirror is broken: are you free?"

The words were spoken close beside her, as she hurried on. She turned; and there, leaning on the parapet in a recess of the bridge, stood Cosmo, in a splendid dress, but with a white and quivering face.

"Cosmo!—I am free—and thy servant for ever. I was coming to you now."

"And I to you, for Death made me bold; but I could get no further. Have I atoned at all? Do I love you a little—truly?"

"Ah, I know now that you love me, my Cosmo; but what do you say about death?"

He did not reply. His hand was pressed against his side. She looked more closely: the blood was welling from between the fingers. She flung her arms around him with a faint bitter wail.

When Lisa came up, she found her mistress kneeling above a wan dead face, which smiled on in the spectral moonbeams.

And now I will say no more about these wondrous volumes; though I could tell many a tale out of them, and could, perhaps, vaguely represent some entrancing thoughts of a deeper kind which I found within them. From many a sultry noon till twilight, did I sit in that grand hall, buried and risen again in these old books. And I trust I have carried away in my soul some of the exhalations of their undying leaves. In after hours of deserved or needful sorrow, portions of what I read there have often come to me again, with an unexpected comforting; which was not fruitless, even though the comfort might seem in itself groundless and vain.

CHAPTER XIV

"Your gallery
Ha we pass'd through, not without much content
In many singularities; but we saw not
That which my daughter came to look upon,
The state of her mother."
                    Winter's Tale.

It seemed to me strange, that all this time I had heard no music in the fairy palace. I was convinced there must be music in it, but that my sense was as yet too gross to receive the influence of those mysterious motions that beget sound. Sometimes I felt sure, from the way the few figures of which I got such transitory glimpses passed me, or glided into vacancy before me, that they were moving to the law of music; and, in fact, several times I fancied for a moment that I heard a few wondrous tones coming I knew not whence. But they did not last long enough to convince me that I had heard them with the bodily sense. Such as they were, however, they took strange liberties with me, causing me to burst suddenly into tears, of which there was no presence to make me ashamed, or casting me into a kind of trance of speechless delight, which, passing as suddenly, left me faint and longing for more.

Now, on an evening, before I had been a week in the palace, I was wandering through one lighted arcade and corridor after another. At length I arrived, through a door that closed behind me, in another vast hall of the palace. It was filled with a subdued crimson light; by which I saw that slender pillars of black, built close to walls of white marble, rose to a great height, and then, dividing into innumerable divergent arches, supported a roof, like the walls, of white marble, upon which the arches intersected intricately, forming a fretting of black upon the white, like the network of a skeleton-leaf. The floor was black.

Between several pairs of the pillars upon every side, the place of the wall behind was occupied by a crimson curtain of thick silk, hanging in heavy and rich folds. Behind each of these curtains burned a powerful light, and these were the sources of the glow that filled the hall. A peculiar delicious odour pervaded the place. As soon as I entered, the old inspiration seemed to return to me, for I felt a strong impulse to sing; or rather, it seemed as if some one else was singing a song in my soul, which wanted to come forth at my lips, imbodied in my breath. But I kept silence; and feeling somewhat overcome by the red light and the perfume, as well as by the emotion within me, and seeing at one end of the hall a great crimson chair, more like a throne than a chair, beside a table of white marble, I went to it, and, throwing myself in it, gave myself up to a succession of images of bewildering beauty, which passed before my inward eye, in a long and occasionally crowded train. Here I sat for hours, I suppose; till, returning somewhat to myself, I saw that the red light had paled away, and felt a cool gentle breath gliding over my forehead. I rose and left the hall with unsteady steps, finding my way with some difficulty to my own chamber, and faintly remembering, as I went, that only in the marble cave, before I found the sleeping statue, had I ever had a similar experience.

After this, I repaired every morning to the same hall; where I sometimes sat in the chair and dreamed deliciously, and sometimes walked up and down over the black floor. Sometimes I acted within myself a whole drama, during one of these perambulations; sometimes walked deliberately through the whole epic of a tale; sometimes ventured to sing a song, though with a shrinking fear of I knew not what. I was astonished at the beauty of my own voice as it rang through the place, or rather crept undulating, like a serpent of sound, along the walls and roof of this superb music-hall. Entrancing verses arose within me as of their own accord, chanting themselves to their own melodies, and requiring no addition of music to satisfy the inward sense. But, ever in the pauses of these, when the singing mood was upon me, I seemed to hear something like the distant sound of multitudes of dancers, and felt as if it was the unheard music, moving their rhythmic motion, that within me blossomed in verse and song. I felt, too, that could I but see the dance, I should, from the harmony of complicated movements, not of the dancers in relation to each other merely, but of each dancer individually in the manifested plastic power that moved the consenting harmonious form, understand the whole of the music on the billows of which they floated and swung.

At length, one night, suddenly, when this feeling of dancing came upon me, I bethought me of lifting one of the crimson curtains, and looking if, perchance, behind it there might not be hid some other mystery, which might at least remove a step further the bewilderment of the present one. Nor was I altogether disappointed. I walked to one of the magnificent draperies, lifted a corner, and peeped in. There, burned a great, crimson, globe-shaped light, high in the cubical centre of another hall, which might be larger or less than that in which I stood, for its dimensions were not easily perceived, seeing that floor and roof and walls were entirely of black marble.

The roof was supported by the same arrangement of pillars radiating in arches, as that of the first hall; only, here, the pillars and arches were of dark red. But what absorbed my delighted gaze, was an innumerable assembly of white marble statues, of every form, and in multitudinous posture, filling the hall throughout. These stood, in the ruddy glow of the great lamp, upon pedestals of jet black. Around the lamp shone in golden letters, plainly legible from where I stood, the two words—

TOUCH NOT!

There was in all this, however, no solution to the sound of dancing; and now I was aware that the influence on my mind had ceased. I did not go in that evening, for I was weary and faint, but I hoarded up the expectation of entering, as of a great coming joy.

Next night I walked, as on the preceding, through the hall. My mind was filled with pictures and songs, and therewith so much absorbed, that I did not for some time think of looking within the curtain I had last night lifted. When the thought of doing so occurred to me first, I happened to be within a few yards of it. I became conscious, at the same moment, that the sound of dancing had been for some time in my ears. I approached the curtain quickly, and, lifting it, entered the black hall. Everything was still as death. I should have concluded that the sound must have proceeded from some other more distant quarter, which conclusion its faintness would, in ordinary circumstances, have necessitated from the first; but there was a something about the statues that caused me still to remain in doubt. As I said, each stood perfectly still upon its black pedestal: but there was about every one a certain air, not of motion, but as if it had just ceased from movement; as if the rest were not altogether of the marbly stillness of thousands of years. It was as if the peculiar atmosphere of each had yet a kind of invisible tremulousness; as if its agitated wavelets had not yet subsided into a perfect calm. I had the suspicion that they had anticipated my appearance, and had sprung, each, from the living joy of the dance, to the death-silence and blackness of its isolated pedestal, just before I entered. I walked across the central hall to the curtain opposite the one I had lifted, and, entering there, found all the appearances similar; only that the statues were different, and differently grouped. Neither did they produce on my mind that impression—of motion just expired, which I had experienced from the others. I found that behind every one of the crimson curtains was a similar hall, similarly lighted, and similarly occupied.

The next night, I did not allow my thoughts to be absorbed as before with inward images, but crept stealthily along to the furthest curtain in the hall, from behind which, likewise, I had formerly seemed to hear the sound of dancing. I drew aside its edge as suddenly as I could, and, looking in, saw that the utmost stillness pervaded the vast place. I walked in, and passed through it to the other end.

There I found that it communicated with a circular corridor, divided from it only by two rows of red columns. This corridor, which was black, with red niches holding statues, ran entirely about the statue-halls, forming a communication between the further ends of them all; further, that is, as regards the central hall of white whence they all diverged like radii, finding their circumference in the corridor.

Round this corridor I now went, entering all the halls, of which there were twelve, and finding them all similarly constructed, but filled with quite various statues, of what seemed both ancient and modern sculpture. After I had simply walked through them, I found myself sufficiently tired to long for rest, and went to my own room.

In the night I dreamed that, walking close by one of the curtains, I was suddenly seized with the desire to enter, and darted in. This time I was too quick for them. All the statues were in motion, statues no longer, but men and women—all shapes of beauty that ever sprang from the brain of the sculptor, mingled in the convolutions of a complicated dance. Passing through them to the further end, I almost started from my sleep on beholding, not taking part in the dance with the others, nor seemingly endued with life like them, but standing in marble coldness and rigidity upon a black pedestal in the extreme left corner—my lady of the cave; the marble beauty who sprang from her tomb or her cradle at the call of my songs. While I gazed in speechless astonishment and admiration, a dark shadow, descending from above like the curtain of a stage, gradually hid her entirely from my view. I felt with a shudder that this shadow was perchance my missing demon, whom I had not seen for days. I awoke with a stifled cry.

Of course, the next evening I began my journey through the halls (for I knew not to which my dream had carried me), in the hope of proving the dream to be a true one, by discovering my marble beauty upon her black pedestal. At length, on reaching the tenth hall, I thought I recognised some of the forms I had seen dancing in my dream; and to my bewilderment, when I arrived at the extreme corner on the left, there stood, the only one I had yet seen, a vacant pedestal. It was exactly in the position occupied, in my dream, by the pedestal on which the white lady stood. Hope beat violently in my heart.

"Now," said I to myself, "if yet another part of the dream would but come true, and I should succeed in surprising these forms in their nightly dance; it might be the rest would follow, and I should see on the pedestal my marble queen. Then surely if my songs sufficed to give her life before, when she lay in the bonds of alabaster, much more would they be sufficient then to give her volition and motion, when she alone of assembled crowds of marble forms, would be standing rigid and cold."

But the difficulty was, to surprise the dancers. I had found that a premeditated attempt at surprise, though executed with the utmost care and rapidity, was of no avail. And, in my dream, it was effected by a sudden thought suddenly executed. I saw, therefore, that there was no plan of operation offering any probability of success, but this: to allow my mind to be occupied with other thoughts, as I wandered around the great centre-hall; and so wait till the impulse to enter one of the others should happen to arise in me just at the moment when I was close to one of the crimson curtains. For I hoped that if I entered any one of the twelve halls at the right moment, that would as it were give me the right of entrance to all the others, seeing they all had communication behind. I would not diminish the hope of the right chance, by supposing it necessary that a desire to enter should awake within me, precisely when I was close to the curtains of the tenth hall.

At first the impulses to see recurred so continually, in spite of the crowded imagery that kept passing through my mind, that they formed too nearly a continuous chain, for the hope that any one of them would succeed as a surprise. But as I persisted in banishing them, they recurred less and less often; and after two or three, at considerable intervals, had come when the spot where I happened to be was unsuitable, the hope strengthened, that soon one might arise just at the right moment; namely, when, in walking round the hall, I should be close to one of the curtains.

At length the right moment and the impulse coincided. I darted into the ninth hall. It was full of the most exquisite moving forms. The whole space wavered and swam with the involutions of an intricate dance. It seemed to break suddenly as I entered, and all made one or two bounds towards their pedestals; but, apparently on finding that they were thoroughly overtaken, they returned to their employment (for it seemed with them earnest enough to be called such) without further heeding me. Somewhat impeded by the floating crowd, I made what haste I could towards the bottom of the hall; whence, entering the corridor, I turned towards the tenth. I soon arrived at the corner I wanted to reach, for the corridor was comparatively empty; but, although the dancers here, after a little confusion, altogether disregarded my presence, I was dismayed at beholding, even yet, a vacant pedestal. But I had a conviction that she was near me. And as I looked at the pedestal, I thought I saw upon it, vaguely revealed as if through overlapping folds of drapery, the indistinct outlines of white feet. Yet there was no sign of drapery or concealing shadow whatever. But I remembered the descending shadow in my dream. And I hoped still in the power of my songs; thinking that what could dispel alabaster, might likewise be capable of dispelling what concealed my beauty now, even if it were the demon whose darkness had overshadowed all my life.

CHAPTER XV

"Alexander. 'When will you finish Campaspe?'
Apelles. 'Never finish: for always in absolute
beauty there is somewhat above art.'"
LYLY'S Campaspe.

And now, what song should I sing to unveil my Isis, if indeed she was present unseen? I hurried away to the white hall of Phantasy, heedless of the innumerable forms of beauty that crowded my way: these might cross my eyes, but the unseen filled my brain. I wandered long, up and down the silent space: no songs came. My soul was not still enough for songs. Only in the silence and darkness of the soul's night, do those stars of the inward firmament sink to its lower surface from the singing realms beyond, and shine upon the conscious spirit. Here all effort was unavailing. If they came not, they could not be found.

Next night, it was just the same. I walked through the red glimmer of the silent hall; but lonely as there I walked, as lonely trod my soul up and down the halls of the brain. At last I entered one of the statue-halls. The dance had just commenced, and I was delighted to find that I was free of their assembly. I walked on till I came to the sacred corner. There I found the pedestal just as I had left it, with the faint glimmer as of white feet still resting on the dead black. As soon as I saw it, I seemed to feel a presence which longed to become visible; and, as it were, called to me to gift it with self-manifestation, that it might shine on me. The power of song came to me. But the moment my voice, though I sang low and soft, stirred the air of the hall, the dancers started; the quick interweaving crowd shook, lost its form, divided; each figure sprang to its pedestal, and stood, a self-evolving life no more, but a rigid, life-like, marble shape, with the whole form composed into the expression of a single state or act. Silence rolled like a spiritual thunder through the grand space. My song had ceased, scared at its own influences. But I saw in the hand of one of the statues close by me, a harp whose chords yet quivered. I remembered that as she bounded past me, her harp had brushed against my arm; so the spell of the marble had not infolded it. I sprang to her, and with a gesture of entreaty, laid my hand on the harp. The marble hand, probably from its contact with the uncharmed harp, had strength enough to relax its hold, and yield the harp to me. No other motion indicated life. Instinctively I struck the chords and sang. And not to break upon the record of my song, I mention here, that as I sang the first four lines, the loveliest feet became clear upon the black pedestal; and ever as I sang, it was as if a veil were being lifted up from before the form, but an invisible veil, so that the statue appeared to grow before me, not so much by evolution, as by infinitesimal degrees of added height. And, while I sang, I did not feel that I stood by a statue, as indeed it appeared to be, but that a real woman-soul was revealing itself by successive stages of imbodiment, and consequent manifestatlon and expression.

> Feet of beauty, firmly planting
>   Arches white on rosy heel!
> Whence the life-spring, throbbing, panting,
>   Pulses upward to reveal!
> Fairest things know least despising;
>   Foot and earth meet tenderly:
> 'Tis the woman, resting, rising
>   Upward to sublimity,
> Rise the limbs, sedately sloping,
>   Strong and gentle, full and free;
> Soft and slow, like certain hoping,
>   Drawing nigh the broad firm knee.
> Up to speech! As up to roses
>   Pants the life from leaf to flower,
> So each blending change discloses,
>   Nearer still, expression's power.
>
> Lo! fair sweeps, white surges, twining
>   Up and outward fearlessly!
> Temple columns, close combining,
>   Lift a holy mystery.
> Heart of mine! what strange surprises
>   Mount aloft on such a stair!
> Some great vision upward rises,
>   Curving, bending, floating fair.
>
> Bands and sweeps, and hill and hollow
>   Lead my fascinated eye;
> Some apocalypse will follow,
>   Some new world of deity.
> Zoned unseen, and outward swelling,
>   With new thoughts and wonders rife,

Queenly majesty foretelling,
  See the expanding house of life!

Sudden heaving, unforbidden
  Sighs eternal, still the same—
Mounts of snow have summits hidden
  In the mists of uttered flame.
But the spirit, dawning nearly
  Finds no speech for earnest pain;
Finds a soundless sighing merely—
  Builds its stairs, and mounts again.

Heart, the queen, with secret hoping,
  Sendeth out her waiting pair;
Hands, blind hands, half blindly groping,
  Half inclasping visions rare;
And the great arms, heartways bending;
  Might of Beauty, drawing home
There returning, and re-blending,
  Where from roots of love they roam.

Build thy slopes of radiance beamy
  Spirit, fair with womanhood!
Tower thy precipice, white-gleamy,
  Climb unto the hour of good.
Dumb space will be rent asunder,
  Now the shining column stands
Ready to be crowned with wonder
  By the builder's joyous hands.

All the lines abroad are spreading,
  Like a fountain's falling race.
Lo, the chin, first feature, treading,
  Airy foot to rest the face!
Speech is nigh; oh, see the blushing,
  Sweet approach of lip and breath!
Round the mouth dim silence, hushing,
  Waits to die ecstatic death.

Span across in treble curving,
  Bow of promise, upper lip!
Set them free, with gracious swerving;

Let the wing-words float and dip.
Dumb art thou? O Love immortal,
  More than words thy speech must be;
Childless yet the tender portal
  Of the home of melody.

Now the nostrils open fearless,
  Proud in calm unconsciousness,
Sure it must be something peerless
  That the great Pan would express!
Deepens, crowds some meaning tender,
  In the pure, dear lady-face.
Lo, a blinding burst of splendour!—
  'Tis the free soul's issuing grace.

Two calm lakes of molten glory
  Circling round unfathomed deeps!
Lightning-flashes, transitory,
  Cross the gulfs where darkness sleeps.
This the gate, at last, of gladness,
  To the outward striving me:
In a rain of light and sadness,
  Out its loves and longings flee!

With a presence I am smitten
  Dumb, with a foreknown surprise;
Presence greater yet than written
  Even in the glorious eyes.
Through the gulfs, with inward gazes,
  I may look till I am lost;
Wandering deep in spirit-mazes,
  In a sea without a coast.

Windows open to the glorious!
  Time and space, oh, far beyond!
Woman, ah! thou art victorious,
  And I perish, overfond.
Springs aloft the yet Unspoken
  In the forehead's endless grace,
Full of silences unbroken;
  Infinite, unfeatured face.

Domes above, the mount of wonder;
  Height and hollow wrapt in night;
Hiding in its caverns under
  Woman-nations in their might.
Passing forms, the highest Human
  Faints away to the Divine
Features none, of man or woman,
  Can unveil the holiest shine.

Sideways, grooved porches only
  Visible to passing eye,
Stand the silent, doorless, lonely
  Entrance-gates of melody.
But all sounds fly in as boldly,
  Groan and song, and kiss and cry
At their galleries, lifted coldly,
  Darkly, 'twixt the earth and sky.

Beauty, thou art spent, thou knowest
  So, in faint, half-glad despair,
From the summit thou o'erflowest
  In a fall of torrent hair;
Hiding what thou hast created
  In a half-transparent shroud:
Thus, with glory soft-abated,
  Shines the moon through vapoury cloud.

CHAPTER XVI

"Ev'n the Styx, which ninefold her infoldeth
  Hems not Ceres' daughter in its flow;
But she grasps the apple—ever holdeth
  Her, sad Orcus, down below."
    SCHILLER, Das Ideal und das Leben.

Ever as I sang, the veil was uplifted; ever as I sang, the signs of life grew; till, when the eyes dawned upon me, it was with that sunrise of splendour which my feeble song attempted to re-imbody.

The wonder is, that I was not altogether overcome, but was able to

93

complete my song as the unseen veil continued to rise. This ability came solely from the state of mental elevation in which I found myself. Only because uplifted in song, was I able to endure the blaze of the dawn. But I cannot tell whether she looked more of statue or more of woman; she seemed removed into that region of phantasy where all is intensely vivid, but nothing clearly defined. At last, as I sang of her descending hair, the glow of soul faded away, like a dying sunset. A lamp within had been extinguished, and the house of life shone blank in a winter morn. She was a statue once more—but visible, and that was much gained. Yet the revulsion from hope and fruition was such, that, unable to restrain myself, I sprang to her, and, in defiance of the law of the place, flung my arms around her, as if I would tear her from the grasp of a visible Death, and lifted her from the pedestal down to my heart. But no sooner had her feet ceased to be in contact with the black pedestal, than she shuddered and trembled all over; then, writhing from my arms, before I could tighten their hold, she sprang into the corridor, with the reproachful cry, "You should not have touched me!" darted behind one of the exterior pillars of the circle, and disappeared. I followed almost as fast; but ere I could reach the pillar, the sound of a closing door, the saddest of all sounds sometimes, fell on my ear; and, arriving at the spot where she had vanished, I saw, lighted by a pale yellow lamp which hung above it, a heavy, rough door, altogether unlike any others I had seen in the palace; for they were all of ebony, or ivory, or covered with silver-plates, or of some odorous wood, and very ornate; whereas this seemed of old oak, with heavy nails and iron studs. Notwithstanding the precipitation of my pursuit, I could not help reading, in silver letters beneath the lamp: "*No one enters here without the leave of the Queen.*" But what was the Queen to me, when I followed my white lady? I dashed the door to the wall and sprang through. Lo! I stood on a waste windy hill. Great stones like tombstones stood all about me. No door, no palace was to be seen. A white figure gleamed past me, wringing her hands, and crying, "Ah! you should have sung to me; you should have sung to me!" and disappeared behind one of the stones. I followed. A cold gust of wind met me from behind the stone; and when I looked, I saw nothing but a great hole in the earth, into which I could find no way of entering. Had she fallen in? I could not tell. I must wait for the daylight. I sat down and wept, for there was no help.

CHAPTER XVII

"First, I thought, almost despairing,
This must crush my spirit now;
Yet I bore it, and am bearing—
Only do not ask me how."
        HEINE.

When the daylight came, it brought the possibility of action, but with it little of consolation. With the first visible increase of light, I gazed into the chasm, but could not, for more than an hour, see sufficiently well to discover its nature. At last I saw it was almost a perpendicular opening, like a roughly excavated well, only very large. I could perceive no bottom; and it was not till the sun actually rose, that I discovered a sort of natural staircase, in many parts little more than suggested, which led round and round the gulf, descending spirally into its abyss. I saw at once that this was my path; and without a moment's hesitation, glad to quit the sunlight, which stared at me most heartlessly, I commenced my tortuous descent. It was very difficult. In some parts I had to cling to the rocks like a bat. In one place, I dropped from the track down upon the next returning spire of the stair; which being broad in this particular portion, and standing out from the wall at right angles, received me upon my feet safe, though somewhat stupefied by the shock. After descending a great way, I found the stair ended at a narrow opening which entered the rock horizontally. Into this I crept, and, having entered, had just room to turn round. I put my head out into the shaft by which I had come down, and surveyed the course of my descent. Looking up, I saw the stars; although the sun must by this time have been high in the heavens. Looking below, I saw that the sides of the shaft went sheer down, smooth as glass; and far beneath me, I saw the reflection of the same stars I had seen in the heavens when I looked up. I turned again, and crept inwards some distance, when the passage widened, and I was at length able to stand and walk upright. Wider and loftier grew the way; new paths branched off on every side; great open halls appeared; till at last I found myself wandering on through an underground country, in which the sky was of rock, and instead of trees and flowers, there were only fantastic rocks and stones. And ever as I went, darker grew my thoughts, till at last I had no hope whatever of finding the white lady: I no longer called her to myself *my* white lady. Whenever a choice was necessary, I always chose the path which seemed to lead downwards.

At length I began to find that these regions were inhabited. From behind a rock a peal of harsh grating laughter, full of evil humour, rang through my ears, and, looking round, I saw a queer, goblin creature, with a great head and ridiculous features, just such as those described, in German histories and travels, as Kobolds. "What do you want with me?" I said. He pointed at me with a long forefinger, very thick at the root, and sharpened to a point, and answered, "He! he! he! what do *you* want here?" Then, changing his tone, he continued, with mock humility— "Honoured sir, vouchsafe to withdraw from thy slaves the lustre of thy august presence, for thy slaves cannot support its brightness." A second appeared, and struck in: "You are so big, you keep the sun from us. We can't see for you, and we're so cold." Thereupon arose, on all sides, the most terrific uproar of laughter, from voices like those of children in volume, but scrannel and harsh as those of decrepit age, though, unfortunately, without its weakness. The whole pandemonium of fairy devils, of all varieties of fantastic ugliness, both in form and feature, and of all sizes from one to four feet, seemed to have suddenly assembled about me. At length, after a great babble of talk among themselves, in a language unknown to me, and after seemingly endless gesticulation, consultation, elbow-nudging, and unmitigated peals of laughter, they formed into a circle about one of their number, who scrambled upon a stone, and, much to my surprise, and somewhat to my dismay, began to sing, in a voice corresponding in its nature to his talking one, from beginning to end, the song with which I had brought the light into the eyes of the white lady. He sang the same air too; and, all the time, maintained a face of mock entreaty and worship; accompanying the song with the travestied gestures of one playing on the lute. The whole assembly kept silence, except at the close of every verse, when they roared, and danced, and shouted with laughter, and flung themselves on the ground, in real or pretended convulsions of delight. When he had finished, the singer threw himself from the top of the stone, turning heels over head several times in his descent; and when he did alight, it was on the top of his head, on which he hopped about, making the most grotesque gesticulations with his legs in the air. Inexpressible laughter followed, which broke up in a shower of tiny stones from innumerable hands. They could not materially injure me, although they cut me on the head and face. I attempted to run away, but they all rushed upon me, and, laying hold of every part that afforded a grasp, held me tight. Crowding about me like bees, they shouted an insect-swarm of exasperating speeches up into my face, among which the most frequently recurring were—"You shan't have her; you shan't have her; he! he! he! She's for a better man; how he'll kiss her! how he'll kiss her!"

The galvanic torrent of this battery of malevolence stung to life within me a spark of nobleness, and I said aloud, "Well, if he is a better man, let him have her."

They instantly let go their hold of me, and fell back a step or two, with a whole broadside of grunts and humphs, as of unexpected and disappointed approbation. I made a step or two forward, and a lane was instantly opened for me through the midst of the grinning little antics, who bowed most politely to me on every side as I passed. After I had gone a few yards, I looked back, and saw them all standing quite still, looking after me, like a great school of boys; till suddenly one turned round, and with a loud whoop, rushed into the midst of the others. In an instant, the whole was one writhing and tumbling heap of contortion, reminding me of the live pyramids of intertwined snakes of which travellers make report. As soon as one was worked out of the mass, he bounded off a few paces, and then, with a somersault and a run, threw himself gyrating into the air, and descended with all his weight on the summit of the heaving and struggling chaos of fantastic figures. I left them still busy at this fierce and apparently aimless amusement. And as I went, I sang—

If a nobler waits for thee,
I will weep aside;
It is well that thou should'st be,
Of the nobler, bride.

For if love builds up the home,
Where the heart is free,
Homeless yet the heart must roam,
That has not found thee.

One must suffer: I, for her
Yield in her my part
Take her, thou art worthier—
Still I be still, my heart!

Gift ungotten! largess high
Of a frustrate will!
But to yield it lovingly
Is a something still.

Then a little song arose of itself in my soul; and I felt for the moment, while it sank sadly within me, as if I was once more walking up and down the white hall of Phantasy in the Fairy Palace. But this lasted no longer than the song; as will be seen.

Do not vex thy violet
Perfume to afford:
Else no odour thou wilt get

From its little hoard.

In thy lady's gracious eyes
Look not thou too long;
Else from them the glory flies,
And thou dost her wrong.

Come not thou too near the maid,
Clasp her not too wild;
Else the splendour is allayed,
And thy heart beguiled.

A crash of laughter, more discordant and deriding than any I had yet heard, invaded my ears. Looking on in the direction of the sound, I saw a little elderly woman, much taller, however, than the goblins I had just left, seated upon a stone by the side of the path. She rose, as I drew near, and came forward to meet me.

She was very plain and commonplace in appearance, without being hideously ugly. Looking up in my face with a stupid sneer, she said: "Isn't it a pity you haven't a pretty girl to walk all alone with you through this sweet country? How different everything would look? wouldn't it? Strange that one can never have what one would like best! How the roses would bloom and all that, even in this infernal hole! wouldn't they, Anodos? Her eyes would light up the old cave, wouldn't they?"

"That depends on who the pretty girl should be," replied I.

"Not so very much matter that," she answered; "look here."

I had turned to go away as I gave my reply, but now I stopped and looked at her. As a rough unsightly bud might suddenly blossom into the most lovely flower; or rather, as a sunbeam bursts through a shapeless cloud, and transfigures the earth; so burst a face of resplendent beauty, as it were *through* the unsightly visage of the woman, destroying it with light as it dawned through it. A summer sky rose above me, gray with heat; across a shining slumberous landscape, looked from afar the peaks of snow-capped mountains; and down from a great rock beside me fell a sheet of water mad with its own delight.

"Stay with me," she said, lifting up her exquisite face, and looking full in mine.

I drew back. Again the infernal laugh grated upon my ears; again the rocks closed in around me, and the ugly woman looked at me with wicked, mocking hazel eyes.

"You shall have your reward," said she. "You shall see your white lady again."

"That lies not with you," I replied, and turned and left her.

She followed me with shriek upon shriek of laughter, as I went on my way.

I may mention here, that although there was always light enough to see my path and a few yards on every side of me, I never could find out the source of this sad sepulchral illumination.

CHAPTER XVIII

"In the wind's uproar, the sea's raging grim,
And the sighs that are born in him."
        HEINE.

"From dreams of bliss shall men awake
One day, but not to weep:
The dreams remain; they only break
The mirror of the sleep."
        JEAN PAUL, Hesperus.

How I got through this dreary part of my travels, I do not know. I do not think I was upheld by the hope that any moment the light might break in upon me; for I scarcely thought about that. I went on with a dull endurance, varied by moments of uncontrollable sadness; for more and more the conviction grew upon me that I should never see the white lady again. It may seem strange that one with whom I had held so little communion should have so engrossed my thoughts; but benefits conferred awaken love in some minds, as surely as benefits received in others. Besides being delighted and proud that *my* songs had called the beautiful creature to life, the same fact caused me to feel a tenderness unspeakable for her, accompanied with a kind of feeling of property in her; for so the goblin Selfishness would reward the angel Love. When to all this is added, an overpowering sense of her beauty, and an unquestioning conviction that this was a true index to inward loveliness, it may be understood how it came to pass that my imagination filled my whole soul with the play of its own multitudinous colours and harmonies around the form which yet stood, a gracious marble radiance, in the midst of *its* white hall of phantasy. The time passed by unheeded; for my thoughts were busy. Perhaps this was also in part the cause of my needing no food, and never thinking how I should find any, during this subterraneous part of my travels. How long they endured I could not tell, for I had no means of measuring time; and when I looked back, there was such a discrepancy between the decisions of my imagination and my judgment, as to the length of time that had passed, that I was bewildered, and gave up all attempts to arrive at any conclusion on the point.

A gray mist continually gathered behind me. When I looked back towards the past, this mist was the medium through which my eyes had to strain for a vision of what had gone by; and the form of the white lady had receded into an unknown region. At length the country of rock began to close again around me, gradually and slowly narrowing, till I found myself walking in a gallery of rock once more, both sides of which I could touch with my outstretched hands. It narrowed yet, until I was forced to move carefully, in order to avoid striking against the projecting pieces of rock. The roof sank lower and lower, until I was compelled, first to stoop, and then to creep on my hands and knees. It recalled terrible dreams of childhood; but I was not much afraid, because I felt sure that this was my path, and my only hope of leaving Fairy Land, of which I was now almost weary.

At length, on getting past an abrupt turn in the passage, through which I had to force myself, I saw, a few yards ahead of me, the long-forgotten daylight shining through a small opening, to which the path, if path it could now be called, led me. With great difficulty I accomplished these last few yards, and came forth to the day. I stood on the shore of a wintry sea, with a wintry sun just a few feet above its horizon-edge. It was bare, and waste, and gray. Hundreds of hopeless waves rushed constantly shorewards, falling exhausted upon a beach of great loose stones, that seemed to stretch miles and miles in both directions. There was nothing for the eye but mingling shades of gray; nothing for the ear but the rush of the coming, the roar of the breaking, and the moan of the retreating wave. No rock lifted up a sheltering severity above the dreariness around; even that from which I had myself emerged rose scarcely a foot above the opening by which I had reached the dismal day, more dismal even than the tomb I had left. A cold, death-like wind swept across the shore, seeming to issue from a pale mouth of cloud upon the horizon. Sign of life was nowhere visible. I wandered over the stones, up and down the beach, a human imbodiment of the nature around me. The wind increased; its keen waves flowed through my soul; the foam rushed higher up the stones; a few dead stars began to gleam in the east; the sound of the waves grew louder and yet more despairing. A dark curtain of cloud was lifted up, and a pale blue rent shone between its foot and the edge of the sea, out from which rushed an icy storm of frozen wind, that tore the waters into spray as it passed, and flung the billows in raving heaps upon the desolate shore. I could bear it no longer.

"I will not be tortured to death," I cried; "I will meet it half-way. The life within me is yet enough to bear me up to the face of Death, and then I die unconquered."

Before it had grown so dark, I had observed, though without any particular interest, that on one part of the shore a low platform of rock seemed to run out far into the midst of the breaking waters.

Towards this I now went, scrambling over smooth stones, to which scarce even a particle of sea-weed clung; and having found it, I got on it, and followed its direction, as near as I could guess, out into the tumbling chaos. I could hardly keep my feet against the wind and sea. The waves repeatedly all but swept me off my path; but I kept on my way, till I reached the end of the low promontory, which, in the fall of the waves, rose a good many feet above the surface, and, in their rise, was covered with their waters. I stood one moment and gazed into the heaving abyss beneath me; then plunged headlong into the mounting wave below. A blessing, like the kiss of a mother, seemed to alight on my soul; a calm, deeper than that which accompanies a hope deferred, bathed my spirit. I sank far into the waters, and sought not to return. I felt as if once more the great arms of the beech-tree were around me, soothing me after the miseries I had passed through, and telling me, like a little sick child, that I should be better to-morrow. The waters of themselves lifted me, as with loving arms, to the surface. I breathed again, but did not unclose my eyes. I would not look on the wintry sea, and the pitiless gray sky. Thus I floated, till something gently touched me. It was a little boat floating beside me. How it came there I could not tell; but it rose and sank on the waters, and kept touching me in its fall, as if with a human will to let me know that help was by me. It was a little gay-coloured boat, seemingly covered with glistering scales like those of a fish, all of brilliant rainbow hues. I scrambled into it, and lay down in the bottom, with a sense of exquisite repose.

Then I drew over me a rich, heavy, purple cloth that was beside me; and, lying still, knew, by the sound of the waters, that my little bark was fleeting rapidly onwards. Finding, however, none of that stormy motion which the sea had manifested when I beheld it from the shore, I opened my eyes; and, looking first up, saw above me the deep violet sky of a warm southern night; and then, lifting my head, saw that I was sailing fast upon a summer sea, in the last border of a southern twilight. The aureole of the sun yet shot the extreme faint tips of its longest rays above the horizon-waves, and withdrew them not. It was a perpetual twilight. The stars, great and earnest, like children's eyes, bent down lovingly towards the waters; and the reflected stars within seemed to float up, as if longing to meet their embraces. But when I looked down, a new wonder met my view. For, vaguely revealed beneath the wave, I floated above my whole Past. The fields of my childhood flitted by; the halls of my youthful labours; the streets of great cities where I had dwelt; and the assemblies of men and women wherein I had wearied myself seeking for rest. But so indistinct were the visions, that sometimes I thought I was sailing on a shallow sea, and that strange rocks and forests of sea-plants beguiled my eye, sufficiently to be transformed, by the magic of the phantasy, into well-known objects and regions. Yet, at times, a beloved form seemed to lie close beneath me in sleep; and the eyelids would tremble as if about to forsake the conscious eye; and the arms would heave upwards, as if in dreams they sought for a satisfying presence. But these motions might come only from the heaving of the waters between those forms and me. Soon I fell asleep, overcome with fatigue and delight. In dreams of unspeakable joy—of restored friendships; of revived embraces; of love which said it had never died; of faces that had vanished long ago, yet said with smiling lips that they knew nothing of the grave; of pardons implored, and granted with such bursting floods of love, that I was almost glad I had sinned—thus I passed through this wondrous twilight. I awoke with the feeling that I had been kissed and loved to my heart's content; and found that my boat was floating motionless by the grassy shore of a little island.

CHAPTER XIX

"In still rest, in changeless simplicity, I bear,
uninterrupted, the consciousness of the whole of Humanity
within me."—SCHLEIERMACHERS, Monologen.

> *"... such a sweetness, such a grace,*
> *In all thy speech appear,*
> *That what to th'eye a beauteous face,*
> *That thy tongue is to the ear."*
> *—COWLEY.*

The water was deep to the very edge; and I sprang from the little boat upon a soft grassy turf. The island seemed rich with a profusion of all grasses and low flowers. All delicate lowly things were most plentiful; but no trees rose skywards, not even a bush overtopped the tall grasses, except in one place near the cottage I am about to describe, where a few plants of the gum-cistus, which drops every night all the blossoms that the day brings forth, formed a kind of natural arbour. The whole island lay open to the sky and sea. It rose nowhere more than a few feet above the level of the waters, which flowed deep all around its border. Here there seemed to be neither tide nor storm. A sense of persistent calm and fulness arose in the mind at the sight of the slow, pulse-like rise and fall of the deep, clear, unrippled waters against the bank of the island, for shore it could hardly be called, being so much more like the edge of a full, solemn river. As I walked over the grass towards the cottage, which stood at a little distance from the bank, all the flowers of childhood looked at me with perfect child-eyes out of the grass. My heart, softened by the dreams through which it had passed, overflowed in a sad, tender love towards them. They looked to me like children impregnably fortified in a helpless confidence. The sun stood half-way down the western sky, shining very soft and golden; and there grew a second world of shadows amidst the world of grasses and wild flowers.

The cottage was square, with low walls, and a high pyramidal roof thatched with long reeds, of which the withered blossoms hung over all the eaves. It is noticeable that most of the buildings I saw in Fairy Land were cottages. There was no path to a door, nor, indeed, was there any track worn by footsteps in the island.

The cottage rose right out of the smooth turf. It had no windows that I could see; but there was a door in the centre of the side facing me, up to which I went. I knocked, and the sweetest voice I had ever heard said, "Come in." I entered. A bright fire was burning on a hearth in the centre of the earthern floor, and the smoke found its way out at an opening in the centre of the pyramidal roof. Over the fire hung a little pot, and over the pot bent a woman-face, the most wonderful, I thought, that I had ever beheld. For it was older than any countenance I had ever looked upon. There was not a spot in which a wrinkle could lie, where a wrinkle lay not. And the skin was ancient and brown, like old parchment. The woman's form was tall and spare: and when she stood up to welcome me, I saw that she was straight as an arrow. Could that voice of sweetness have issued from those lips of age? Mild as they were, could they be the portals whence flowed such melody? But the moment I saw her eyes, I no longer wondered at her voice: they were absolutely young—those of a woman of five-and-twenty, large, and of a clear gray. Wrinkles had beset them all about; the eyelids themselves were old, and heavy, and worn; but the eyes were very incarnations of soft light. She held out her hand to me, and the voice of sweetness again greeted me, with the single word, "Welcome." She set an old wooden chair for me, near the fire, and went on with her cooking. A wondrous sense of refuge and repose came upon me. I felt like a boy who has got home from school, miles across the hills, through a heavy storm of wind and snow. Almost, as I gazed on her, I sprang from my seat to kiss those old lips. And when, having finished her cooking, she brought some of the dish she had prepared, and set it on a little table by me, covered with a snow-white cloth, I could not help laying my head on her bosom, and bursting into happy tears. She put her arms round me, saying, "Poor child; poor child!"

As I continued to weep, she gently disengaged herself, and, taking a spoon, put some of the food (I did not know what it was) to my lips, entreating me most endearingly to swallow it. To please her, I made an effort, and succeeded. She went on feeding me like a baby, with one arm round me, till I looked up in her face and smiled: then she gave me the spoon and told me to eat, for it would do me good. I obeyed her, and found myself wonderfully refreshed. Then she drew near the fire an old-fashioned couch that was in the cottage, and making me lie down upon it, sat at my feet, and began to sing. Amazing store of old ballads rippled from her lips, over the pebbles of ancient tunes; and the voice that sang was sweet as the voice of a tuneful maiden that singeth ever from very fulness of song. The songs were almost all sad, but with a sound of comfort. One I can faintly recall. It was something like this:

> Sir Aglovaile through the churchyard rode;
>> Sing, All alone I lie:
> Little recked he where'er he yode,
>> All alone, up in the sky.
>
> Swerved his courser, and plunged with fear
>> All alone i lie:
> His cry might have wakened the dead men near,
>> All alone, up in the sky.
>
> The very dead that lay at his feet,
> Lapt in the mouldy winding-sheet.
>
> But he curbed him and spurred him, until he stood
> Still in his place, like a horse of wood,
>
> With nostrils uplift, and eyes wide and wan;
> But the sweat in streams from his fetlocks ran.
>
> A ghost grew out of the shadowy air,
> And sat in the midst of her moony hair.
>
> In her gleamy hair she sat and wept;

In the dreamful moon they lay and slept;

The shadows above, and the bodies below,
Lay and slept in the moonbeams slow.

And she sang, like the moan of an autumn wind
Over the stubble left behind:

Alas, how easily things go wrong!
A sigh too much, or a kiss too long,
And there follows a mist and a weeping rain,
And life is never the same again.

Alas, how hardly things go right!
'Tis hard to watch on a summer night,
For the sigh will come and the kiss will stay,
And the summer night is a winter day.

"Oh, lovely ghosts my heart is woes
To see thee weeping and wailing so.

Oh, lovely ghost," said the fearless knight,
"Can the sword of a warrior set it right?

Or prayer of bedesman, praying mild,
As a cup of water a feverish child,

Sooth thee at last, in dreamless mood
To sleep the sleep a dead lady should?

Thine eyes they fill me with longing sore,
As if I had known thee for evermore.

Oh, lovely ghost, I could leave the day
To sit with thee in the moon away

If thou wouldst trust me, and lay thy head
To rest on a bosom that is not dead."
The lady sprang up with a strange ghost-cry,
And she flung her white ghost-arms on high:

And she laughed a laugh that was not gay,

And it lengthened out till it died away;

And the dead beneath turned and moaned,
And the yew-trees above they shuddered and groaned.

"Will he love me twice with a love that is vain?
Will he kill the poor ghost yet again?

I thought thou wert good; but I said, and wept:
'Can I have dreamed who have not slept?'

And I knew, alas! or ever I would,
Whether I dreamed, or thou wert good.

When my baby died, my brain grew wild.
I awoke, and found I was with my child."

"If thou art the ghost of my Adelaide,
How is it? Thou wert but a village maid,

And thou seemest an angel lady white,
Though thin, and wan, and past delight."

The lady smiled a flickering smile,
And she pressed her temples hard the while.

"Thou seest that Death for a woman can
Do more than knighthood for a man."

"But show me the child thou callest mine,
Is she out to-night in the ghost's sunshine?"

"In St. Peter's Church she is playing on,
At hide-and-seek, with Apostle John.

When the moonbeams right through the window go,
Where the twelve are standing in glorious show,

She says the rest of them do not stir,
But one comes down to play with her.

Then I can go where I list, and weep,

For good St. John my child will keep."

"Thy beauty filleth the very air,
   Never saw I a woman so fair."

"Come, if thou darest, and sit by my side;
   But do not touch me, or woe will betide.

Alas, I am weak: I might well know
   This gladness betokens some further woe.

Yet come. It will come. I will bear it. I can.
   For thou lovest me yet—though but as a man."

The knight dismounted in earnest speed;
   Away through the tombstones thundered the steed,

And fell by the outer wall, and died.
   But the knight he kneeled by the lady's side;

Kneeled beside her in wondrous bliss,
   Rapt in an everlasting kiss:

Though never his lips come the lady nigh,
   And his eyes alone on her beauty lie.

All the night long, till the cock crew loud,
   He kneeled by the lady, lapt in her shroud.

And what they said, I may not say:
   Dead night was sweeter than living day.

How she made him so blissful glad
   Who made her and found her so ghostly sad,

I may not tell; but it needs no touch
   To make them blessed who love so much.

"Come every night, my ghost, to me;
   And one night I will come to thee.

'Tis good to have a ghostly wife:

She will not tremble at clang of strife;

She will only hearken, amid the din,
Behind the door, if he cometh in."

And this is how Sir Aglovaile
Often walked in the moonlight pale.

And oft when the crescent but thinned the gloom,
Full orbed moonlight filled his room;

And through beneath his chamber door,
Fell a ghostly gleam on the outer floor;

And they that passed, in fear averred
That murmured words they often heard.

'Twas then that the eastern crescent shone
Through the chancel window, and good St. John

Played with the ghost-child all the night,
And the mother was free till the morning light,

And sped through the dawning night, to stay
With Aglovaile till the break of day.

And their love was a rapture, lone and high,
And dumb as the moon in the topmost sky.

One night Sir Aglovaile, weary, slept
And dreamed a dream wherein he wept.

A warrior he was, not often wept he,
But this night he wept full bitterly.

He woke—beside him the ghost-girl shone
Out of the dark: 'twas the eve of St. John.

He had dreamed a dream of a still, dark wood,
Where the maiden of old beside him stood;

But a mist came down, and caught her away,

And he sought her in vain through the pathless day,

Till he wept with the grief that can do no more,
And thought he had dreamt the dream before.

From bursting heart the weeping flowed on;
And lo! beside him the ghost-girl shone;

Shone like the light on a harbour's breast,
Over the sea of his dream's unrest;

Shone like the wondrous, nameless boon,
That the heart seeks ever, night or noon:

Warnings forgotten, when needed most,
He clasped to his bosom the radiant ghost.

She wailed aloud, and faded, and sank.
With upturn'd white face, cold and blank,

In his arms lay the corpse of the maiden pale,
And she came no more to Sir Aglovaile.

Only a voice, when winds were wild,
Sobbed and wailed like a chidden child.

Alas, how easily things go wrong!
A sigh too much, or a kiss too long,
And there follows a mist and a weeping rain,
And life is never the same again.

This was one of the simplest of her songs, which, perhaps, is the cause of my being able to remember it better than most of the others. While she sung, I was in Elysium, with the sense of a rich soul upholding, embracing, and overhanging mine, full of all plenty and bounty. I felt as if she could give me everything I wanted; as if I should never wish to leave her, but would be content to be sung to and fed by her, day after day, as years rolled by. At last I fell asleep while she sang.

When I awoke, I knew not whether it was night or day. The fire had sunk to a few red embers, which just gave light enough to show me the woman standing a few feet from me, with her back towards me, facing the door by which I had entered. She was weeping, but very gently and plentifully. The tears seemed to come freely from her heart. Thus she stood for a few minutes; then, slowly turning at right angles to her former position, she faced another of the four sides of the cottage. I now observed, for the first time, that here was a door likewise; and that, indeed, there was one in the centre of every side of the cottage.

When she looked towards the second door, her tears ceased to flow, but sighs took their place. She often closed her eyes as she stood; and every time she closed her eyes, a gentle sigh seemed to be born in her heart, and to escape at her lips. But when her eyes were open, her sighs were deep and very sad, and shook her whole frame. Then she turned towards the third door, and a cry as of fear or suppressed pain broke from her; but she seemed to hearten herself against the dismay, and to front it steadily; for, although I often heard a slight cry, and sometimes a moan, yet she never moved or bent her head, and I felt sure that her eyes never closed. Then she turned to the fourth door, and I saw her shudder, and then stand still as a statue; till at last she turned towards me and approached the fire. I saw that her face was white as death. But she gave one look upwards, and smiled the sweetest, most child-innocent smile; then heaped fresh wood on the fire, and, sitting down by the blaze, drew her wheel near her, and began to spin. While she spun, she murmured a low strange song, to which the hum of the wheel made a kind of infinite symphony. At length she paused in her spinning and singing, and glanced towards me, like a mother who looks whether or not her child gives signs of waking. She smiled when she saw that my eyes were open. I asked her whether it was day yet. She answered, "It is always day here, so long as I keep my fire burning."

I felt wonderfully refreshed; and a great desire to see more of the island awoke within me. I rose, and saying that I wished to look about me, went towards the door by which I had entered.

"Stay a moment," said my hostess, with some trepidation in her voice. "Listen to me. You will not see what you expect when you go out of that door. Only remember this: whenever you wish to come back to me, enter wherever you see this mark."

She held up her left hand between me and the fire. Upon the palm, which appeared almost transparent, I saw, in dark red, a mark like this —> which I took care to fix in my mind.

She then kissed me, and bade me good-bye with a solemnity that awed me; and bewildered me too, seeing I was only going out for a little ramble in an island, which I did not believe larger than could easily be compassed in a few hours' walk at most. As I went she resumed her spinning.

I opened the door, and stepped out. The moment my foot touched the smooth sward, I seemed to issue from the door of an old barn on my father's estate, where, in the hot afternoons, I used to go and lie amongst the straw, and read. It seemed to me now that I had been asleep there. At a little distance in the field, I saw two of my brothers at play. The moment they caught sight of me, they called out to me to come and join them, which I did; and we played together as we had done years ago, till the red sun went down in the west, and the gray fog began to rise from the river. Then we went home together with a strange happiness. As we went, we heard the continually renewed larum of a landrail in the long grass. One of my brothers and I separated to a little distance, and each commenced running towards the part whence the sound appeared to come, in the hope of approaching the spot where the bird was, and so getting at least a sight of it, if we should not be able to capture the little creature. My father's voice recalled us from trampling down the rich long grass, soon to be cut down and laid aside for the winter. I had quite forgotten all about Fairy Land, and the wonderful old woman, and the curious red mark.

My favourite brother and I shared the same bed. Some childish dispute arose between us; and our last words, ere we fell asleep, were not of kindness, notwithstanding the pleasures of the day. When I woke in the morning, I missed him. He had risen early, and had gone to bathe in the river. In another hour, he was brought home drowned. Alas! alas! if we had only gone to sleep as usual, the one with his arm about the other! Amidst the horror of the moment, a strange conviction flashed across my mind, that I had gone through the very same once before.

I rushed out of the house, I knew not why, sobbing and crying bitterly. I ran through the fields in aimless distress, till, passing the old barn, I caught sight of a red mark on the door. The merest trifles sometimes rivet the attention in the deepest misery; the intellect has so little to do with grief. I went up to look at this mark, which I did not remember ever to have seen before. As I looked at it, I thought I would go in and lie down amongst the straw, for I was very weary with running about and weeping. I opened the door; and there in the cottage sat the old woman as I had left her, at her spinning-wheel.

"I did not expect you quite so soon," she said, as I shut the door behind me. I went up to the couch, and threw myself on it with that fatigue wherewith one awakes from a feverish dream of hopeless grief.

The old woman sang:

The great sun, benighted,
May faint from the sky;
But love, once uplighted,
Will never more die.

Form, with its brightness,
From eyes will depart:
It walketh, in whiteness,
The halls of the heart.

Ere she had ceased singing, my courage had returned. I started from the couch, and, without taking leave of the old woman, opened the door of Sighs, and sprang into what should appear.

I stood in a lordly hall, where, by a blazing fire on the hearth, sat a lady, waiting, I knew, for some one long desired. A mirror was near me, but I saw that my form had no place within its depths, so I feared not that I should be seen. The lady wonderfully resembled my marble lady, but was altogether of the daughters of men, and I could not tell whether or not it was she.

It was not for me she waited. The tramp of a great horse rang through the court without. It ceased, and the clang of armour told that his rider alighted, and the sound of his ringing heels approached the hall. The door opened; but the lady waited, for she would meet her lord alone. He strode in: she flew like a home-bound dove into his arms, and nestled on the hard steel. It was the knight of the soiled armour. But now the armour shone like polished glass; and strange to tell, though the mirror reflected not my form, I saw a dim shadow of myself in the shining steel. "O my beloved, thou art come, and I am blessed."

Her soft fingers speedily overcame the hard clasp of his helmet; one by one she undid the buckles of his armour; and she toiled under the weight of the mail, as she *would* carry it aside. Then she unclasped his greaves, and unbuckled his spurs; and once more she sprang into his arms, and laid her head where she could now feel the beating of his heart. Then she disengaged herself from his embrace, and, moving back a step or two, gazed at him. He stood there a mighty form, crowned with a noble head, where all sadness had disappeared, or had been absorbed in solemn purpose. Yet I suppose that he looked more thoughtful than the lady had expected to see him, for she did not renew her caresses, although his face glowed with love, and the few words he spoke were as mighty deeds for strength; but she led him towards the hearth, and seated him in an ancient chair, and set wine before him, and sat at his feet.

"I am sad," he said, "when I think of the youth whom I met twice in the forests of Fairy Land; and who, you say, twice, with his songs, roused you from the death-sleep of an evil enchantment. There was something noble in him, but it was a nobleness of thought, and not of deed. He may yet perish of vile fear."

"Ah!" returned the lady, "you saved him once, and for that I thank you; for may I not say that I somewhat loved him? But tell me how you fared, when you struck your battle-axe into the ash-tree, and he came and found you; for so much of the story you had told me, when the beggar-child came and took you away."

"As soon as I saw him," rejoined the knight, "I knew that earthly arms availed not against such as he; and that my soul must meet him in its naked strength. So I unclasped my helm, and flung it on the ground; and, holding my good axe yet in my hand, gazed at him with steady eyes. On he came, a horror indeed, but I did not flinch. Endurance must conquer, where force could not reach. He came nearer and nearer, till the ghastly face was close to mine. A shudder as of death ran through me; but I think I did not move, for he seemed to quail, and retreated. As soon as he gave back, I struck one more sturdy blow on the stem of his tree, that the forest rang; and then looked at him again. He writhed and grinned with rage and apparent pain, and again approached me, but retreated sooner than before. I heeded him no more, but hewed with a will at the tree, till the trunk creaked, and the head bowed, and with a crash it fell to the earth. Then I looked up from my labour, and lo! the spectre had vanished, and I saw him no more; nor ever in my wanderings have I heard of him again."

"Well struck! well withstood! my hero," said the lady.

"But," said the knight, somewhat troubled, "dost thou love the youth still?"

"Ah!" she replied, "how can I help it? He woke me from worse than death; he loved me. I had never been for thee, if he had not sought me first. But I love him not as I love thee. He was but the moon of my night; thou art the sun of my day, O beloved."

"Thou art right," returned the noble man. "It were hard, indeed, not to have some love in return for such a gift as he hath given thee. I, too, owe him more than words can speak."

Humbled before them, with an aching and desolate heart, I yet could not restrain my words:

"Let me, then, be the moon of thy night still, O woman! And when thy day is beclouded, as the fairest days will be, let some song of mine comfort thee, as an old, withered, half-forgotten thing, that belongs to an ancient mournful hour of uncompleted birth, which yet was beautiful in its time."

They sat silent, and I almost thought they were listening. The colour of the lady's eyes grew deeper and deeper; the slow tears grew, and filled them, and overflowed. They rose, and passed, hand in hand, close to where I stood; and each looked towards me in passing. Then they disappeared through a door which closed behind them; but, ere it closed, I saw that the room into which it opened was a rich chamber, hung with gorgeous arras. I stood with an ocean of sighs frozen in my bosom. I could remain no longer. She was near me, and I could not see her; near me in the arms of one loved better than I, and I would not see her, and I would not be by her. But how to escape from the nearness of the best beloved? I had not this time forgotten the mark; for the fact that I could not enter the sphere of these living beings kept me aware that, for me, I moved in a vision, while they moved in life. I looked all about for the mark, but could see it nowhere; for I avoided looking just where it was. There the dull red cipher glowed, on the very door of their secret chamber. Struck with agony, I dashed it open, and fell at the feet of the ancient woman, who still spun on, the whole dissolved ocean of my sighs bursting from me in a storm of tearless sobs. Whether I fainted or slept, I do not know; but, as I returned to consciousness, before I seemed to have power to move, I heard the woman singing, and could distinguish the words:

> *O light of dead and of dying days!*
>   *O Love! in thy glory go,*
> *In a rosy mist and a moony maze,*
>   *O'er the pathless peaks of snow.*
>
> *But what is left for the cold gray soul,*
>   *That moans like a wounded dove?*
> *One wine is left in the broken bowl!—*
>   *'Tis—To love, and love and love.*

Now I could weep. When she saw me weeping, she sang:

> *Better to sit at the waters' birth,*
>   *Than a sea of waves to win;*
> *To live in the love that floweth forth,*
>   *Than the love that cometh in.*
>
> *Be thy heart a well of love, my child,*
>   *Flowing, and free, and sure;*
> *For a cistern of love, though undefiled,*
>   *Keeps not the spirit pure.*

I rose from the earth, loving the white lady as I had never loved her before.

Then I walked up to the door of Dismay, and opened it, and went out. And lo! I came forth upon a crowded street, where men and women went to and fro in multitudes. I knew it well; and, turning to one hand, walked sadly along the pavement. Suddenly I saw approaching me, a little way off, a form well known to me (*well-known!*—alas, how weak the word!) in the years when I thought my boyhood was left behind, and shortly before I entered the realm of Fairy Land. Wrong and Sorrow had gone together, hand-in-hand as it is well they do.

Unchangeably dear was that face. It lay in my heart as a child lies in its own white bed; but I could not meet her.

"Anything but that," I said, and, turning aside, sprang up the steps to a door, on which I fancied I saw the mystic sign. I entered—not the mysterious cottage, but her home. I rushed wildly on, and stood by the door of her room.

"She is out," I said, "I will see the old room once more."

I opened the door gently, and stood in a great solemn church. A deep-toned bell, whose sounds throbbed and echoed and swam through the empty building, struck the hour of midnight. The moon shone through the windows of the clerestory, and enough of the ghostly radiance was diffused through the church to let me see, walking with a stately, yet somewhat trailing and stumbling step, down the opposite aisle, for I stood in one of the transepts, a figure dressed in a white robe, whether for the night, or for that longer night which lies too deep for the day, I could not tell. Was it she? and was this her chamber? I crossed the church, and followed. The figure stopped, seemed to ascend as it were a high bed, and lay down. I reached the place where it lay, glimmering white. The bed was a tomb. The light was too ghostly to see clearly, but I passed my hand over the face and the hands and the feet, which were all bare. They were cold—they were marble, but I knew them. It grew dark. I turned to retrace my steps, but found, ere long, that I had wandered into what seemed a little chapel. I groped about, seeking the door. Everything I touched belonged to the dead. My hands fell on the cold effigy of a knight who lay with his legs crossed and his sword broken beside him. He lay in his noble rest, and I lived on in ignoble strife. I felt for the left hand and a certain finger; I found there the ring I knew: he was one of my own ancestors. I was in the chapel over the burial-vault of my race. I called aloud: "If any of the dead are moving here, let them take pity upon me, for I, alas! am still alive; and let some dead woman comfort me, for I am a stranger in the land of the dead, and see no light." A warm kiss alighted on my lips through the dark. And I said, "The dead kiss well; I will not be afraid." And a great hand was reached out of the dark, and grasped mine for a moment, mightily and tenderly. I said to myself: "The veil between, though very dark, is very thin."

Groping my way further, I stumbled over the heavy stone that covered the entrance of the vault: and, in stumbling, descried upon the stone the mark, glowing in red fire. I caught the great ring. All my effort could not have moved the huge slab; but it opened the door of the cottage, and I threw myself once more, pale and speechless, on the couch beside the ancient dame. She sang once more:

> Thou dreamest: on a rock thou art,
>   High o'er the broken wave;
> Thou fallest with a fearful start
>   But not into thy grave;
> For, waking in the morning's light,
> Thou smilest at the vanished night
>
> So wilt thou sink, all pale and dumb,
>   Into the fainting gloom;
> But ere the coming terrors come,
>   Thou wak'st—where is the tomb?
> Thou wak'st—the dead ones smile above,
> With hovering arms of sleepless love.

She paused; then sang again:

> We weep for gladness, weep for grief;
>   The tears they are the same;
> We sigh for longing, and relief;
>   The sighs have but one name,
>
> And mingled in the dying strife,
>   Are moans that are not sad
> The pangs of death are throbs of life,
>   Its sighs are sometimes glad.
>
> The face is very strange and white:
>   It is Earth's only spot
> That feebly flickers back the light
>   The living seeth not.

I fell asleep, and slept a dreamless sleep, for I know not how long. When I awoke, I found that my hostess had moved from where she had been sitting, and now sat between me and the fourth door.

I guessed that her design was to prevent my entering there. I sprang from the couch, and darted past her to the door. I opened it at once and went out. All I remember is a cry of distress from the woman: "Don't go there, my child! Don't go there!" But I was gone.

I knew nothing more; or, if I did, I had forgot it all when I awoke to consciousness, lying on the floor of the cottage, with my head in the lap of the woman, who was weeping over me, and stroking my hair with both hands, talking to me as a mother might talk to a sick and sleeping, or a dead child. As soon as I looked up and saw her, she smiled through her tears; smiled with withered face and young eyes, till her countenance was irradiated with the light of the smile. Then she bathed my head and face and hands in an icy cold, colourless liquid, which smelt a little of damp earth. Immediately I was able to sit up. She rose and put some food before me. When I had eaten, she said: "Listen to me, my child. You must leave me directly!"

"Leave you!" I said. "I am so happy with you. I never was so happy in my life."

"But you must go," she rejoined sadly. "Listen! What do you hear?"

"I hear the sound as of a great throbbing of water."

"Ah! you do hear it? Well, I had to go through that door—the door of the Timeless" (and she shuddered as she pointed to the fourth door)—"to find you; for if I had not gone, you would never have entered again; and because I went, the waters around my cottage will rise and rise, and flow and come, till they build a great firmament of waters over my dwelling. But as long as I keep my fire burning, they cannot enter. I have fuel enough for years; and after one year they will sink away again, and be just as they were before you came. I have not been buried for a hundred years now." And she smiled and wept.

"Alas! alas!" I cried. "I have brought this evil on the best and kindest of friends, who has filled my heart with great gifts."

"Do not think of that," she rejoined. "I can bear it very well. You will come back to me some day, I know. But I beg you, for my sake, my dear child, to do one thing. In whatever sorrow you may be, however inconsolable and irremediable it may appear, believe me that the old woman in the cottage, with the young eyes" (and she smiled), "knows something, though she must not always tell it, that would quite satisfy you about it, even in the worst moments of your distress. Now you must go."

"But how can I go, if the waters are all about, and if the doors all lead into other regions and other worlds?"

"This is not an island," she replied; "but is joined to the land by a narrow neck; and for the door, I will lead you myself through the right one."

She took my hand, and led me through the third door; whereupon I found myself standing in the deep grassy turf on which I had landed from the little boat, but upon the opposite side of the cottage. She pointed out the direction I must take, to find the isthmus and escape the rising waters.

Then putting her arms around me, she held me to her bosom; and as I kissed her, I felt as if I were leaving my mother for the first time, and could not help weeping bitterly. At length she gently pushed me away, and with the words, "Go, my son, and do something worth doing," turned back, and, entering the cottage, closed the door behind her. I felt very desolate as I went.

CHAPTER XX

"Thou hadst no fame; that which thou didst like good
Was but thy appetite that swayed thy blood
For that time to the best; for as a blast
That through a house comes, usually doth cast
Things out of order, yet by chance may come
And blow some one thing to his proper room,
So did thy appetite, and not thy zeal,
Sway thee by chance to do some one thing well."
FLETCHER'S Faithful Shepherdess.

"The noble hart that harbours vertuous thought
And is with childe of glorious great intent,
Can never rest, until it forth have brought
Th' eternall brood of glorie excellent."
SPENSER, The Faerie Queene.

I had not gone very far before I felt that the turf beneath my feet was soaked with the rising waters. But I reached the isthmus in safety. It was rocky, and so much higher than the level of the peninsula, that I had plenty of time to cross. I saw on each side of me the water rising rapidly, altogether without wind, or violent motion, or broken waves, but as if a slow strong fire were glowing beneath it. Ascending a steep acclivity, I found myself at last in an open, rocky country. After travelling for some hours, as nearly in a straight line as I could, I arrived at a lonely tower, built on the top of a little hill, which overlooked the whole neighbouring country. As I approached, I heard the clang of an anvil; and so rapid were the blows, that I despaired of making myself heard till a pause in the work should ensue. It was some minutes before a cessation took place; but when it did, I knocked loudly, and had not long to wait; for, a moment after, the door was partly opened by a noble-looking youth, half-undressed, glowing with heat, and begrimed with the blackness of the forge. In one hand he held a sword, so lately from the furnace that it yet shone with a dull fire. As soon as he saw me, he threw the door wide open, and standing aside, invited me very cordially to enter. I did so; when he shut and bolted the door most carefully, and then led the way inwards. He brought me into a rude hall, which seemed to occupy almost the whole of the ground floor of the little tower, and which I saw was now being used as a workshop. A huge fire roared on the hearth, beside which was an anvil. By the anvil stood, in similar undress, and in a waiting attitude, hammer in hand, a second youth, tall as the former, but far more slightly built. Reversing the usual course of perception in such meetings, I thought them, at first sight, very unlike; and at the second glance, knew that they were brothers. The former, and apparently the elder, was muscular and dark, with curling hair, and large hazel eyes, which sometimes grew wondrously soft. The second was slender and fair, yet with a countenance like an eagle, and an eye which, though pale blue, shone with an almost fierce expression. He stood erect, as if looking from a lofty mountain crag, over a vast plain outstretched below. As soon as we entered the hall, the elder turned to me, and I saw that a glow of satisfaction shone on both their faces. To my surprise and great pleasure, he addressed me thus:

"Brother, will you sit by the fire and rest, till we finish this part of our work?"

I signified my assent; and, resolved to await any disclosure they might be inclined to make, seated myself in silence near the hearth.

The elder brother then laid the sword in the fire, covered it well over, and when it had attained a sufficient degree of heat, drew it out and laid it on the anvil, moving it carefully about, while the younger, with a succession of quick smart blows, appeared either to be welding it, or hammering one part of it to a consenting shape with the rest. Having finished, they laid it carefully in the fire; and, when it was very hot indeed, plunged it into a vessel full of some liquid, whence a blue flame sprang upwards, as the glowing steel entered.

There they left it; and drawing two stools to the fire, sat down, one on each side of me.

"We are very glad to see you, brother. We have been expecting you for some days," said the dark-haired youth.

"I am proud to be called your brother," I rejoined; "and you will not think I refuse the name, if I desire to know why you honour me with it?"

"Ah! then he does not know about it," said the younger. "We thought you had known of the bond betwixt us, and the work we have to do together. You must tell him, brother, from the first."

So the elder began:

"Our father is king of this country. Before we were born, three giant brothers had appeared in the land. No one knew exactly when, and no one had the least idea whence they came. They took possession of a ruined castle that had stood unchanged and unoccupied within the memory of any of the country people. The vaults of this castle had remained uninjured by time, and these, I presume, they made use of at first. They were rarely seen, and never offered the least injury to any one; so that they were regarded in the neighbourhood as at least perfectly harmless, if not rather benevolent beings. But it began to be observed, that the old castle had assumed somehow or other, no one knew when or how, a somewhat different look from what it used to have. Not only were several breaches in the lower part of the walls built up, but actually some of the battlements which yet stood, had been repaired, apparently to prevent them from falling into worse decay, while the more important parts were being restored. Of course, every one supposed the giants must have a hand in the work, but no one ever saw them engaged in it. The peasants became yet more uneasy, after one, who had concealed himself, and watched all night, in the neighbourhood of the castle, reported that he had seen, in full moonlight, the three huge giants working with might and main, all night long, restoring to their former position some massive stones, formerly steps of a grand turnpike stair, a great portion of which had long since fallen, along with part of the wall of the round tower in which it had been built. This wall they were completing, foot by foot, along with the stair. But the people said they had no just pretext for interfering: although the real reason for letting the giants alone was, that everybody was far too much afraid of them to interrupt them.

"At length, with the help of a neighbouring quarry, the whole of the external wall of the castle was finished. And now the country folks were in greater fear than before. But for several years the giants remained very peaceful. The reason of this was afterwards supposed to be the fact, that they were distantly related to several good people in the country; for, as long as these lived, they remained quiet; but as soon as they were all dead the real nature of the giants broke out. Having completed the outside of their castle, they proceeded, by spoiling the country houses around them, to make a quiet luxurious provision for their comfort within. Affairs reached such a pass, that the news of their robberies came to my father's ears; but he, alas! was so crippled in his resources, by a war he was carrying on with a neighbouring prince, that he could only spare a very few men, to attempt the capture of their stronghold. Upon these the giants issued in the night, and slew every man of them. And now, grown bolder by success and impunity, they no longer confined their depredations to property, but began to seize the persons of their distinguished neighbours, knights and ladies, and hold them in durance, the misery of which was heightened by all manner of indignity, until they were redeemed by their friends, at an exorbitant ransom. Many knights have adventured their overthrow, but to their own instead; for they have all been slain, or captured, or forced to make a hasty retreat. To crown their enormities, if any man now attempts their destruction, they, immediately upon his defeat, put one or more of their captives to a shameful death, on a turret in sight of all passers-by; so that they have been much less molested of late; and we, although we have burned, for years, to attack these demons and destroy them, dared not, for the sake of their captives, risk the adventure, before we should have reached at least our earliest manhood. Now, however, we are preparing for the attempt; and the grounds of this preparation are these. Having only the resolution, and not the experience necessary for the undertaking, we went and consulted a lonely woman of wisdom, who lives not very far from here, in the direction of the quarter from which you have come. She received us most kindly, and gave us what seems to us the best of advice. She first inquired what experience we had had in arms. We told her we had been well exercised from our boyhood, and for some years had kept ourselves in constant practice, with a view to this necessity.

"'But you have not actually fought for life and death?' said she.

"We were forced to confess we had not.

"'So much the better in some respects,' she replied. 'Now listen to me. Go first and work with an armourer, for as long time as you find needful to obtain a knowledge of his craft; which will not be long, seeing your hearts will be all in the work. Then go to some lonely tower, you two alone. Receive no visits from man or woman. There forge for yourselves every piece of armour that you wish to wear, or to use, in your coming encounter. And keep up your exercises. As, however, two of you can be no match for the three giants, I will find you, if I can, a third brother, who will take on himself the third share of the fight, and the preparation. Indeed, I have already seen one who will, I think, be the very man for your fellowship, but it will be some time before he comes to me. He is wandering now without an aim. I will show him to you in a glass, and, when he comes, you will know him at once. If he will share your endeavours, you must teach him all you know, and he will repay you well, in present song, and in future deeds.'

"She opened the door of a curious old cabinet that stood in the room. On the inside of this door was an oval convex mirror. Looking in it for some time, we at length saw reflected the place where we stood, and the old dame seated in her chair. Our forms were not reflected. But at the feet of the dame lay a young man, yourself, weeping.

"'Surely this youth will not serve our ends,' said I, 'for he weeps.'
"The old woman smiled. 'Past tears are present strength,' said she.
"'Oh!' said my brother, 'I saw you weep once over an eagle you shot.'
"'That was because it was so like you, brother,' I replied; 'but indeed, this youth may have better cause for tears than that—I was wrong.'
"'Wait a while,' said the woman; 'if I mistake not, he will make you weep till your tears are dry for ever. Tears are the only cure for weeping. And you may have need of the cure, before you go forth to fight the giants. You must wait for him, in your tower, till he comes.'
"Now if you will join us, we will soon teach you to make your armour; and we will fight together, and work together, and love each other as never three loved before. And you will sing to us, will you not?"
"That I will, when I can," I answered; "but it is only at times that the power of song comes upon me. For that I must wait; but I have a feeling that if I work well, song will not be far off to enliven the labour."
This was all the compact made: the brothers required nothing more, and I did not think of giving anything more. I rose, and threw off my upper garments.
"I know the uses of the sword," I said. "I am ashamed of my white hands beside yours so nobly soiled and hard; but that shame will soon be wiped away."
"No, no; we will not work to-day. Rest is as needful as toil. Bring the wine, brother; it is your turn to serve to-day."
The younger brother soon covered a table with rough viands, but good wine; and we ate and drank heartily, beside our work. Before the meal was over, I had learned all their story. Each had something in his heart which made the conviction, that he would victoriously perish in the coming conflict, a real sorrow to him. Otherwise they thought they would have lived enough. The causes of their trouble were respectively these:
While they wrought with an armourer, in a city famed for workmanship in steel and silver, the elder had fallen in love with a lady as far beneath him in real rank, as she was above the station he had as apprentice to an armourer. Nor did he seek to further his suit by discovering himself; but there was simply so much manhood about him, that no one ever thought of rank when in his company. This is what his brother said about it. The lady could not help loving him in return. He told her when he left her, that he had a perilous adventure before him, and that when it was achieved, she would either see him return to claim her, or hear that he had died with honour. The younger brother's grief arose from the fact, that, if they were both slain, his old father, the king, would be childless. His love for his father was so exceeding, that to one unable to

sympathise with it, it would have appeared extravagant. Both loved him equally at heart; but the love of the younger had been more developed, because his thoughts and anxieties had not been otherwise occupied. When at home, he had been his constant companion; and, of late, had ministered to the infirmities of his growing age. The youth was never weary of listening to the tales of his sire's youthful adventures; and had not yet in the smallest degree lost the conviction, that his father was the greatest man in the world. The grandest triumph possible to his conception was, to return to his father, laden with the spoils of one of the hated giants. But they both were in some dread, lest the thought of the loneliness of these two might occur to them, in the moment when decision was most necessary, and disturb, in some degree, the self-possession requisite for the success of their attempt. For, as I have said, they were yet untried in actual conflict. "Now," thought I, "I see to what the powers of my gift must minister." For my own part, I did not dread death, for I had nothing to care to live for; but I dreaded the encounter because of the responsibility connected with it. I resolved however to work hard, and thus grow cool, and quick, and forceful.

The time passed away in work and song, in talk and ramble, in friendly fight and brotherly aid. I would not forge for myself armour of heavy mail like theirs, for I was not so powerful as they, and depended more for any success I might secure, upon nimbleness of motion, certainty of eye, and ready response of hand. Therefore I began to make for myself a shirt of steel plates and rings; which work, while more troublesome, was better suited to me than the heavier labour. Much assistance did the brothers give me, even after, by their instructions, I was able to make some progress alone. Their work was in a moment abandoned, to render any required aid to mine. As the old woman had promised, I tried to repay them with song; and many were the tears they both shed over my ballads and dirges. The songs they liked best to hear were two which I made for them. They were not half so good as many others I knew, especially some I had learned from the wise woman in the cottage; but what comes nearest to our needs we like the best.

1   The king sat on his throne
       Glowing in gold and red;
    The crown in his right hand shone,
       And the gray hairs crowned his head.

    His only son walks in,
       And in walls of steel he stands:
    Make me, O father, strong to win,
       With the blessing of holy hands."

He knelt before his sire,
 Who blessed him with feeble smile
His eyes shone out with a kingly fire,
 But his old lips quivered the while.

"Go to the fight, my son,
 Bring back the giant's head;
And the crown with which my brows have done,
 Shall glitter on thine instead."

"My father, I seek no crowns,
 But unspoken praise from thee;
For thy people's good, and thy renown,
 I will die to set them free."

The king sat down and waited there,
 And rose not, night nor day;
Till a sound of shouting filled the air,
 And cries of a sore dismay.

Then like a king he sat once more,
 With the crown upon his head;
And up to the throne the people bore
 A mighty giant dead.

And up to the throne the people bore
 A pale and lifeless boy.
The king rose up like a prophet of yore,
 In a lofty, deathlike joy.

He put the crown on the chilly brow:
 "Thou should'st have reigned with me
But Death is the king of both, and now
 I go to obey with thee.

"Surely some good in me there lay,
 To beget the noble one."
The old man smiled like a winter day,
 And fell beside his son.

II   "O lady, thy lover is dead," they cried;

"He is dead, but hath slain the foe;
He hath left his name to be magnified
In a song of wonder and woe."

"Alas! I am well repaid," said she,
"With a pain that stings like joy:
For I feared, from his tenderness to me,
That he was but a feeble boy.

"Now I shall hold my head on high,
The queen among my kind;
If ye hear a sound, 'tis only a sigh
For a glory left behind."

The first three times I sang these songs they both wept passionately. But after the third time, they wept no more. Their eyes shone, and their faces grew pale, but they never wept at any of my songs again.

CHAPTER XXI

"I put my life in my hands."—The Book of Judges.

At length, with much toil and equal delight, our armour was finished. We armed each other, and tested the strength of the defence, with many blows of loving force. I was inferior in strength to both my brothers, but a little more agile than either; and upon this agility, joined to precision in hitting with the point of my weapon, I grounded my hopes of success in the ensuing combat. I likewise laboured to develop yet more the keenness of sight with which I was naturally gifted; and, from the remarks of my companions, I soon learned that my endeavours were not in vain.

The morning arrived on which we had determined to make the attempt, and succeed or perish—perhaps both. We had resolved to fight on foot; knowing that the mishap of many of the knights who had made the attempt, had resulted from the fright of their horses at the appearance of the giants; and believing with Sir Gawain, that, though mare's sons might be false to us, the earth would never prove a traitor. But most of our preparations were, in their immediate aim at least, frustrated.

We rose, that fatal morning, by daybreak. We had rested from all labour the day before, and now were fresh as the lark. We bathed in cold spring water, and dressed ourselves in clean garments, with a sense of preparation, as for a solemn festivity. When we had broken our fast, I took an old lyre, which I had found in the tower and had myself repaired, and sung for the last time the two ballads of which I have said so much already. I followed them with this, for a closing song:

> *Oh, well for him who breaks his dream*
> > *With the blow that ends the strife*
> *And, waking, knows the peace that flows*
> > *Around the pain of life!*

> *We are dead, my brothers! Our bodies clasp,*
> > *As an armour, our souls about;*
> *This hand is the battle-axe I grasp,*
> > *And this my hammer stout.*

> *Fear not, my brothers, for we are dead;*
> > *No noise can break our rest;*
> *The calm of the grave is about the head,*
> > *And the heart heaves not the breast.*

> *And our life we throw to our people back,*
> > *To live with, a further store;*
> *We leave it them, that there be no lack*
> > *In the land where we live no more.*

> *Oh, well for him who breaks his dream*
> > *With the blow that ends the strife*
> *And, waking, knows the peace that flows*
> > *Around the noise of life!*

As the last few tones of the instrument were following, like a dirge, the death of the song, we all sprang to our feet. For, through one of the little windows of the tower, towards which I had looked as I sang, I saw, suddenly rising over the edge of the slope on which our tower stood, three enormous heads. The brothers knew at once, by my looks, what caused my sudden movement. We were utterly unarmed, and there was no time to arm.

But we seemed to adopt the same resolution simultaneously; for each caught up his favourite weapon, and, leaving his defence behind, sprang to the door. I snatched up a long rapier, abruptly, but very finely pointed, in my sword-hand, and in the other a sabre; the elder brother seized his heavy battle-axe; and the younger, a great, two-handed sword, which he wielded in one hand like a feather. We had just time to get clear of the tower, embrace and say good-bye, and part to some little distance, that we might not encumber each other's motions, ere the triple giant-brotherhood drew near to attack us. They were about twice our height, and armed to the teeth. Through the visors of their helmets their monstrous eyes shone with a horrible ferocity. I was in the middle position, and the middle giant approached me. My eyes were busy with his armour, and I was not a moment in settling my mode of attack. I saw that his body-armour was somewhat clumsily made, and that the overlappings in the lower part had more play than necessary; and I hoped that, in a fortunate moment, some joint would open a little, in a visible and accessible part. I stood till he came near enough to aim a blow at me with the mace, which has been, in all ages, the favourite weapon of giants, when, of course, I leaped aside, and let the blow fall upon the spot where I had been standing. I expected this would strain the joints of his armour yet more. Full of fury, he made at me again; but I kept him busy, constantly eluding his blows, and hoping thus to fatigue him. He did not seem to fear any assault from me, and I attempted none as yet; but while I watched his motions in order to avoid his blows, I, at the same time, kept equal watch upon those joints of his armour, through some one of which I hoped to reach his life. At length, as if somewhat fatigued, he paused a moment, and drew himself slightly up; I bounded forward, foot and hand, ran my rapier right through to the armour of his back, let go the hilt, and passing under his right arm, turned as he fell, and flew at him with my sabre. At one happy blow I divided the band of his helmet, which fell off, and allowed me, with a second cut across the eyes, to blind him quite; after which I clove his head, and turned, uninjured, to see how my brothers had fared. Both the giants were down, but so were my brothers. I flew first to the one and then to the other couple. Both pairs of combatants were dead, and yet locked together, as in the death-struggle. The elder had buried his battle-axe in the body of his foe, and had fallen beneath him as he fell. The giant had strangled him in his own death-agonies. The younger had nearly hewn off the left leg of his enemy; and, grappled with in the act, had, while they rolled together on the earth, found for his dagger a passage betwixt the gorget and cuirass of the giant, and stabbed him mortally in the throat. The blood from the giant's throat was yet pouring over the hand of his foe, which still grasped the hilt of the dagger sheathed in the wound. They lay silent. I, the least worthy, remained the sole survivor in the lists.

As I stood exhausted amidst the dead, after the first worthy deed of my life, I suddenly looked behind me, and there lay the Shadow, black in the sunshine. I went into the lonely tower, and there lay the useless armour of the noble youths—supine as they.

Ah, how sad it looked! It was a glorious death, but it was death. My songs could not comfort me now. I was almost ashamed that I was alive, when they, the true-hearted, were no more. And yet I breathed freer to think that I had gone through the trial, and had not failed. And perhaps I may be forgiven, if some feelings of pride arose in my bosom, when I looked down on the mighty form that lay dead by my hand.

"After all, however," I said to myself, and my heart sank, "it was only skill. Your giant was but a blunderer."

I left the bodies of friends and foes, peaceful enough when the death-fight was over, and, hastening to the country below, roused the peasants. They came with shouting and gladness, bringing waggons to carry the bodies. I resolved to take the princes home to their father, each as he lay, in the arms of his country's foe. But first I searched the giants, and found the keys of their castle, to which I repaired, followed by a great company of the people. It was a place of wonderful strength. I released the prisoners, knights and ladies, all in a sad condition, from the cruelties and neglects of the giants. It humbled me to see them crowding round me with thanks, when in truth the glorious brothers, lying dead by their lonely tower, were those to whom the thanks belonged. I had but aided in carrying out the thought born in their brain, and uttered in visible form before ever I laid hold thereupon. Yet I did count myself happy to have been chosen for their brother in this great deed.

After a few hours spent in refreshing and clothing the prisoners, we all commenced our journey towards the capital. This was slow at first; but, as the strength and spirits of the prisoners returned, it became more rapid; and in three days we reached the palace of the king. As we entered the city gates, with the huge bulks lying each on a waggon drawn by horses, and two of them inextricably intertwined with the dead bodies of their princes, the people raised a shout and then a cry, and followed in multitudes the solemn procession.

I will not attempt to describe the behaviour of the grand old king. Joy and pride in his sons overcame his sorrow at their loss. On me he heaped every kindness that heart could devise or hand execute. He used to sit and question me, night after night, about everything that was in any way connected with them and their preparations. Our mode of life, and relation to each other, during the time we spent together, was a constant theme. He entered into the minutest details of the construction of the armour, even to a peculiar mode of riveting some of the plates, with unwearying interest. This armour I had intended to beg of the king, as my sole memorials of the contest; but, when I saw the delight he took in contemplating it, and the consolation it appeared to afford him in his sorrow, I could not ask for it; but, at his request, left my own, weapons and all, to be joined with theirs in a trophy, erected in the grand square of the palace. The king, with gorgeous ceremony, dubbed me knight with his own old hand, in which trembled the sword of his youth.

During the short time I remained, my company was, naturally, much courted by the young nobles. I was in a constant round of gaiety and diversion, notwithstanding that the court was in mourning. For the country was so rejoiced at the death of the giants, and so many of their lost friends had been restored to the nobility and men of wealth, that the gladness surpassed the grief. "Ye have indeed left your lives to your people, my great brothers!" I said.

But I was ever and ever haunted by the old shadow, which I had not seen all the time that I was at work in the tower. Even in the society of the ladies of the court, who seemed to think it only their duty to make my stay there as pleasant to me as possible, I could not help being conscious of its presence, although it might not be annoying me at the time. At length, somewhat weary of uninterrupted pleasure, and nowise strengthened thereby, either in body or mind, I put on a splendid suit of armour of steel inlaid with silver, which the old king had given me, and, mounting the horse on which it had been brought to me, took my leave of the palace, to visit the distant city in which the lady dwelt, whom the elder prince had loved. I anticipated a sore task, in conveying to her the news of his glorious fate: but this trial was spared me, in a manner as strange as anything that had happened to me in Fairy Land.

CHAPTER XXII

"No one has my form but the I."
Schoppe, in JEAN PAUL'S Titan.

"Joy's a subtil elf.
I think man's happiest when he forgets himself."
CYRIL TOURNEUR, The Revenger's Tragedy.

On the third day of my journey, I was riding gently along a road, apparently little frequented, to judge from the grass that grew upon it. I was approaching a forest. Everywhere in Fairy Land forests are the places where one may most certainly expect adventures. As I drew near, a youth, unarmed, gentle, and beautiful, who had just cut a branch from a yew growing on the skirts of the wood, evidently to make himself a bow, met me, and thus accosted me:

"Sir knight, be careful as thou ridest through this forest; for it is said to be strangely enchanted, in a sort which even those who have been witnesses of its enchantment can hardly describe."

I thanked him for his advice, which I promised to follow, and rode on. But the moment I entered the wood, it seemed to me that, if enchantment there was, it must be of a good kind; for the Shadow, which had been more than usually dark and distressing, since I had set out on this journey, suddenly disappeared. I felt a wonderful elevation of spirits, and began to reflect on my past life, and especially on my combat with the giants, with such satisfaction, that I had actually to remind myself, that I had only killed one of them; and that, but for the brothers, I should never have had the idea of attacking them, not to mention the smallest power of standing to it. Still I rejoiced, and counted myself amongst the glorious knights of old; having even the unspeakable presumption—my shame and self-condemnation at the memory of it are such, that I write it as the only and sorest penance I can perform—to think of myself (will the world believe it?) as side by side with Sir Galahad! Scarcely had the thought been born in my mind, when, approaching me from the left, through the trees, I espied a resplendent knight, of mighty size, whose armour seemed to shine of itself, without the sun. When he drew near, I was astonished to see that this armour was like my own; nay, I could trace, line for line, the correspondence of the inlaid silver to the device on my own. His horse, too, was like mine in colour, form, and motion; save that, like his rider, he was greater and fiercer than his counterpart. The knight rode with beaver up. As he halted right opposite to me in the narrow path, barring my way, I saw the reflection of my countenance in the centre plate of shining steel on his breastplate. Above it rose the same face—his face—only, as I have said, larger and fiercer. I was bewildered. I could not help feeling some admiration of him, but it was mingled with a dim conviction that he was evil, and that I ought to fight with him.

"Let me pass," I said.

"When I will," he replied.

Something within me said: "Spear in rest, and ride at him! else thou art for ever a slave."

I tried, but my arm trembled so much, that I could not couch my lance. To tell the truth, I, who had overcome the giant, shook like a coward before this knight. He gave a scornful laugh, that echoed through the wood, turned his horse, and said, without looking round, "Follow me." I obeyed, abashed and stupefied. How long he led, and how long I followed, I cannot tell. "I never knew misery before," I said to myself.

"Would that I had at least struck him, and had had my death-blow in return! Why, then, do I not call to him to wheel and defend himself? Alas! I know not why, but I cannot. One look from him would cow me like a beaten hound." I followed, and was silent.

At length we came to a dreary square tower, in the middle of a dense forest. It looked as if scarce a tree had been cut down to make room for it. Across the very door, diagonally, grew the stem of a tree, so large that there was just room to squeeze past it in order to enter. One miserable square hole in the roof was the only visible suggestion of a window. Turret or battlement, or projecting masonry of any kind, it had none. Clear and smooth and massy, it rose from its base, and ended with a line straight and unbroken. The roof, carried to a centre from each of the four walls, rose slightly to the point where the rafters met. Round the base lay several little heaps of either bits of broken branches, withered and peeled, or half-whitened bones; I could not distinguish which. As I approached, the ground sounded hollow beneath my horse's hoofs. The knight took a great key from his pocket, and reaching past the stem of the tree, with some difficulty opened the door. "Dismount," he commanded. I obeyed. He turned my horse's head away from the tower, gave him a terrible blow with the flat side of his sword, and sent him madly tearing through the forest.

"Now," said he, "enter, and take your companion with you."

I looked round: knight and horse had vanished, and behind me lay the horrible shadow. I entered, for I could not help myself; and the shadow followed me. I had a terrible conviction that the knight and he were one. The door closed behind me.

Now I was indeed in pitiful plight. There was literally nothing in the tower but my shadow and me. The walls rose right up to the roof; in which, as I had seen from without, there was one little square opening. This I now knew to be the only window the tower possessed. I sat down on the floor, in listless wretchedness. I think I must have fallen asleep, and have slept for hours; for I suddenly became aware of existence, in observing that the moon was shining through the hole in the roof. As she rose higher and higher, her light crept down the wall over me, till at last it shone right upon my head. Instantaneously the walls of the tower seemed to vanish away like a mist. I sat beneath a beech, on the edge of a forest, and the open country lay, in the moonlight, for miles and miles around me, spotted with glimmering houses and spires and towers. I thought with myself, "Oh, joy! it was only a dream; the horrible narrow waste is gone, and I wake beneath a beech-tree, perhaps one that loves me, and I can go where I will." I rose, as I thought, and walked about, and did what I would, but ever kept near the tree; for always, and, of

131

course, since my meeting with the woman of the beech-tree far more than ever, I loved that tree. So the night wore on. I waited for the sun to rise, before I could venture to renew my journey. But as soon as the first faint light of the dawn appeared, instead of shining upon me from the eye of the morning, it stole like a fainting ghost through the little square hole above my head; and the walls came out as the light grew, and the glorious night was swallowed up of the hateful day. The long dreary day passed. My shadow lay black on the floor. I felt no hunger, no need of food. The night came. The moon shone. I watched her light slowly descending the wall, as I might have watched, adown the sky, the long, swift approach of a helping angel. Her rays touched me, and I was free. Thus night after night passed away. I should have died but for this. Every night the conviction returned, that I was free. Every morning I sat wretchedly disconsolate. At length, when the course of the moon no longer permitted her beams to touch me, the night was dreary as the day.

When I slept, I was somewhat consoled by my dreams; but all the time I dreamed, I knew that I was only dreaming. But one night, at length, the moon, a mere shred of pallor, scattered a few thin ghostly rays upon me; and I think I fell asleep and dreamed. I sat in an autumn night before the vintage, on a hill overlooking my own castle. My heart sprang with joy. Oh, to be a child again, innocent, fearless, without shame or desire! I walked down to the castle. All were in consternation at my absence. My sisters were weeping for my loss. They sprang up and clung to me, with incoherent cries, as I entered. My old friends came flocking round me. A gray light shone on the roof of the hall. It was the light of the dawn shining through the square window of my tower. More earnestly than ever, I longed for freedom after this dream; more drearily than ever, crept on the next wretched day. I measured by the sunbeams, caught through the little window in the trap of my tower, how it went by, waiting only for the dreams of the night.

About noon, I started as if something foreign to all my senses and all my experience, had suddenly invaded me; yet it was only the voice of a woman singing. My whole frame quivered with joy, surprise, and the sensation of the unforeseen. Like a living soul, like an incarnation of Nature, the song entered my prison-house. Each tone folded its wings, and laid itself, like a caressing bird, upon my heart. It bathed me like a sea; inwrapt me like an odorous vapour; entered my soul like a long draught of clear spring-water; shone upon me like essential sunlight; soothed me like a mother's voice and hand. Yet, as the clearest forest-well tastes sometimes of the bitterness of decayed leaves, so to my weary, prisoned heart, its cheerfulness had a sting of cold, and its tenderness unmanned me with the faintness of long-departed joys. I wept half-bitterly, half-luxuriously; but not long. I dashed away the tears, ashamed of a weakness which I thought I had abandoned. Ere I knew, I had walked to the door, and seated myself with my ears against it, in order to catch every syllable of the revelation from the unseen outer world. And now I heard each word distinctly. The singer seemed to be standing or sitting near the tower, for the sounds indicated no change of place. The song was something like this:

The sun, like a golden knot on high,
Gathers the glories of the sky,
And binds them into a shining tent,
Roofing the world with the firmament.
And through the pavilion the rich winds blow,
And through the pavilion the waters go.
And the birds for joy, and the trees for prayer,
Bowing their heads in the sunny air,
And for thoughts, the gently talking springs,
That come from the centre with secret things—
All make a music, gentle and strong,
Bound by the heart into one sweet song.
And amidst them all, the mother Earth
Sits with the children of her birth;
She tendeth them all, as a mother hen
Her little ones round her, twelve or ten:
Oft she sitteth, with hands on knee,
Idle with love for her family.
Go forth to her from the dark and the dust,
And weep beside her, if weep thou must;
If she may not hold thee to her breast,
Like a weary infant, that cries for rest
At least she will press thee to her knee,
And tell a low, sweet tale to thee,
Till the hue to thy cheeky and the light to thine eye,
Strength to thy limbs, and courage high
To thy fainting heart, return amain,
And away to work thou goest again.
From the narrow desert, O man of pride,
Come into the house, so high and wide.

Hardly knowing what I did, I opened the door. Why had I not done so before? I do not know.

At first I could see no one; but when I had forced myself past the tree which grew across the entrance, I saw, seated on the ground, and leaning against the tree, with her back to my prison, a beautiful woman. Her countenance seemed known to me, and yet unknown. She looked at me and smiled, when I made my appearance.

"Ah! were you the prisoner there? I am very glad I have wiled you out." "Do you know me then?" "Do you not know me? But you hurt me, and that, I suppose, makes it easy for a man to forget. You broke my globe. Yet I thank you. Perhaps I owe you many thanks for breaking it. I took the pieces, all black, and wet with crying over them, to the Fairy Queen. There was no music and no light in them now. But she took them from me, and laid them aside; and made me go to sleep in a great hall of white, with black pillars, and many red curtains. When I woke in the morning, I went to her, hoping to have my globe again, whole and sound; but she sent me away without it, and I have not seen it since. Nor do I care for it now. I have something so much better. I do not need the globe to play to me; for I can sing. I could not sing at all before. Now I go about everywhere through Fairy Land, singing till my heart is like to break, just like my globe, for very joy at my own songs. And wherever I go, my songs do good, and deliver people. And now I have delivered you, and I am so happy."

She ceased, and the tears came into her eyes.

All this time, I had been gazing at her; and now fully recognised the face of the child, glorified in the countenance of the woman.

I was ashamed and humbled before her; but a great weight was lifted from my thoughts. I knelt before her, and thanked her, and begged her to forgive me.

"Rise, rise," she said; "I have nothing to forgive; I thank you. But now I must be gone, for I do not know how many may be waiting for me, here and there, through the dark forests; and they cannot come out till I come."

She rose, and with a smile and a farewell, turned and left me. I dared not ask her to stay; in fact, I could hardly speak to her. Between her and me, there was a great gulf. She was uplifted, by sorrow and well-doing, into a region I could hardly hope ever to enter. I watched her departure, as one watches a sunset. She went like a radiance through the dark wood, which was henceforth bright to me, from simply knowing that such a creature was in it.

She was bearing the sun to the unsunned spots. The light and the music of her broken globe were now in her heart and her brain. As she went, she sang; and I caught these few words of her song; and the tones seemed to linger and wind about the trees after she had disappeared:

> Thou goest thine, and I go mine—
> Many ways we wend;

Many days, and many ways,
Ending in one end.

Many a wrong, and its curing song;
Many a road, and many an inn;
Room to roam, but only one home
For all the world to win.

And so she vanished. With a sad heart, soothed by humility, and the knowledge of her peace and gladness, I bethought me what now I should do. First, I must leave the tower far behind me, lest, in some evil moment, I might be once more caged within its horrible walls. But it was ill walking in my heavy armour; and besides I had now no right to the golden spurs and the resplendent mail, fitly dulled with long neglect. I might do for a squire; but I honoured knighthood too highly, to call myself any longer one of the noble brotherhood. I stripped off all my armour, piled it under the tree, just where the lady had been seated, and took my unknown way, eastward through the woods. Of all my weapons, I carried only a short axe in my hand.

Then first I knew the delight of being lowly; of saying to myself, "I am what I am, nothing more." "I have failed," I said, "I have lost myself— would it had been my shadow." I looked round: the shadow was nowhere to be seen. Ere long, I learned that it was not myself, but only my shadow, that I had lost. I learned that it is better, a thousand-fold, for a proud man to fall and be humbled, than to hold up his head in his pride and fancied innocence. I learned that he that will be a hero, will barely be a man; that he that will be nothing but a doer of his work, is sure of his manhood. In nothing was my ideal lowered, or dimmed, or grown less precious; I only saw it too plainly, to set myself for a moment beside it. Indeed, my ideal soon became my life; whereas, formerly, my life had consisted in a vain attempt to behold, if not my ideal in myself, at least myself in my ideal. Now, however, I took, at first, what perhaps was a mistaken pleasure, in despising and degrading myself. Another self seemed to arise, like a white spirit from a dead man, from the dumb and trampled self of the past. Doubtless, this self must again die and be buried, and again, from its tomb, spring a winged child; but of this my history as yet bears not the record.

Self will come to life even in the slaying of self; but there is ever something deeper and stronger than it, which will emerge at last from the unknown abysses of the soul: will it be as a solemn gloom, burning with eyes? or a clear morning after the rain? or a smiling child, that finds itself nowhere, and everywhere?

CHAPTER XXIII

"High erected thought, seated in a heart of courtesy."
SIR PHILIP SIDNEY.

"A sweet attractive kinde of grace,
A full assurance given by lookes,
Continuall comfort in a face,
The lineaments of Gospel bookes."
MATTHEW ROYDON, on Sir Philip Sidney.

I had not gone far, for I had but just lost sight of the hated tower, when a voice of another sort, sounding near or far, as the trees permitted or intercepted its passage, reached me. It was a full, deep, manly voice, but withal clear and melodious. Now it burst on the ear with a sudden swell, and anon, dying away as suddenly, seemed to come to me across a great space. Nevertheless, it drew nearer; till, at last, I could distinguish the words of the song, and get transient glimpses of the singer, between the columns of the trees. He came nearer, dawning upon me like a growing thought. He was a knight, armed from head to heel, mounted upon a strange-looking beast, whose form I could not understand. The words which I heard him sing were like these:

Heart be stout,
And eye be true;
Good blade out!
And ill shall rue.

Courage, horse!
Thou lackst no skill;
Well thy force
Hath matched my will.

For the foe
With fiery breath,
At a blow,
Is still in death.

Gently, horse!
Tread fearlessly;

'Tis his corse
That burdens thee.

The sun's eye
Is fierce at noon;
Thou and I
Will rest full soon.

And new strength
New work will meet;
Till, at length,
Long rest is sweet.

And now horse and rider had arrived near enough for me to see, fastened by the long neck to the hinder part of the saddle, and trailing its hideous length on the ground behind, the body of a great dragon. It was no wonder that, with such a drag at his heels, the horse could make but slow progress, notwithstanding his evident dismay. The horrid, serpent-like head, with its black tongue, forked with red, hanging out of its jaws, dangled against the horse's side. Its neck was covered with long blue hair, its sides with scales of green and gold. Its back was of corrugated skin, of a purple hue. Its belly was similar in nature, but its colour was leaden, dashed with blotches of livid blue. Its skinny, bat-like wings and its tail were of a dull gray. It was strange to see how so many gorgeous colours, so many curving lines, and such beautiful things as wings and hair and scales, combined to form the horrible creature, intense in ugliness.

The knight was passing me with a salutation; but, as I walked towards him, he reined up, and I stood by his stirrup. When I came near him, I saw to my surprise and pleasure likewise, although a sudden pain, like a birth of fire, sprang up in my heart, that it was the knight of the soiled armour, whom I knew before, and whom I had seen in the vision, with the lady of the marble. But I could have thrown my arms around him, because she loved him. This discovery only strengthened the resolution I had formed, before I recognised him, of offering myself to the knight, to wait upon him as a squire, for he seemed to be unattended. I made my request in as few words as possible. He hesitated for a moment, and looked at me thoughtfully. I saw that he suspected who I was, but that he continued uncertain of his suspicion. No doubt he was soon convinced of its truth; but all the time I was with him, not a word crossed his lips with reference to what he evidently concluded I wished to leave unnoticed, if not to keep concealed.

"Squire and knight should be friends," said he: "can you take me by the hand?" And he held out the great gauntleted right hand. I grasped it willingly and strongly. Not a word more was said. The knight gave the sign to his horse, which again began his slow march, and I walked beside and a little behind.

We had not gone very far before we arrived at a little cottage; from which, as we drew near, a woman rushed out with the cry:

"My child! my child! have you found my child?"

"I have found her," replied the knight, "but she is sorely hurt. I was forced to leave her with the hermit, as I returned. You will find her there, and I think she will get better. You see I have brought you a present. This wretch will not hurt you again." And he undid the creature's neck, and flung the frightful burden down by the cottage door.

The woman was now almost out of sight in the wood; but the husband stood at the door, with speechless thanks in his face.

"You must bury the monster," said the knight. "If I had arrived a moment later, I should have been too late. But now you need not fear, for such a creature as this very rarely appears, in the same part, twice during a lifetime."

"Will you not dismount and rest you, Sir Knight?" said the peasant, who had, by this time, recovered himself a little.

"That I will, thankfully," said he; and, dismounting, he gave the reins to me, and told me to unbridle the horse, and lead him into the shade. "You need not tie him up," he added; "he will not run away."

When I returned, after obeying his orders, and entered the cottage, I saw the knight seated, without his helmet, and talking most familiarly with the simple host. I stood at the open door for a moment, and, gazing at him, inwardly justified the white lady in preferring him to me. A nobler countenance I never saw. Loving-kindness beamed from every line of his face. It seemed as if he would repay himself for the late arduous combat, by indulging in all the gentleness of a womanly heart. But when the talk ceased for a moment, he seemed to fall into a reverie. Then the exquisite curves of the upper lip vanished. The lip was lengthened and compressed at the same moment. You could have told that, within the lips, the teeth were firmly closed. The whole face grew stern and determined, all but fierce; only the eyes burned on like a holy sacrifice, uplift on a granite rock.

The woman entered, with her mangled child in her arms. She was pale as her little burden. She gazed, with a wild love and despairing tenderness, on the still, all but dead face, white and clear from loss of blood and terror.

The knight rose. The light that had been confined to his eyes, now shone from his whole countenance. He took the little thing in his arms, and, with the mother's help, undressed her, and looked to her wounds. The tears flowed down his face as he did so. With tender hands he bound them up, kissed the pale cheek, and gave her back to her mother. When he went home, all his tale would be of the grief and joy of the parents; while to me, who had looked on, the gracious countenance of the armed man, beaming from the panoply of steel, over the seemingly dead child, while the powerful hands turned it and shifted it, and bound it, if possible even more gently than the mother's, formed the centre of the story.

After we had partaken of the best they could give us, the knight took his leave, with a few parting instructions to the mother as to how she should treat the child.

I brought the knight his steed, held the stirrup while he mounted, and then followed him through the wood. The horse, delighted to be free of his hideous load, bounded beneath the weight of man and armour, and could hardly be restrained from galloping on. But the knight made him time his powers to mine, and so we went on for an hour or two. Then the knight dismounted, and compelled me to get into the saddle, saying: "Knight and squire must share the labour."

Holding by the stirrup, he walked along by my side, heavily clad as he was, with apparent ease. As we went, he led a conversation, in which I took what humble part my sense of my condition would permit me.

"Somehow or other," said he, "notwithstanding the beauty of this country of Faerie, in which we are, there is much that is wrong in it. If there are great splendours, there are corresponding horrors; heights and depths; beautiful women and awful fiends; noble men and weaklings. All a man has to do, is to better what he can. And if he will settle it with himself, that even renown and success are in themselves of no great value, and be content to be defeated, if so be that the fault is not his; and so go to his work with a cool brain and a strong will, he will get it done; and fare none the worse in the end, that he was not burdened with provision and precaution."

"But he will not always come off well," I ventured to say.

"Perhaps not," rejoined the knight, "in the individual act; but the result of his lifetime will content him."

"So it will fare with you, doubtless," thought I; "but for me——"

Venturing to resume the conversation after a pause, I said, hesitatingly:

"May I ask for what the little beggar-girl wanted your aid, when she came to your castle to find you?"

He looked at me for a moment in silence, and then said—

"I cannot help wondering how you know of that; but there is something about you quite strange enough to entitle you to the privilege of the country; namely, to go unquestioned. I, however, being only a man, such as you see me, am ready to tell you anything you like to ask me, as far as I can. The little beggar-girl came into the hall where I was sitting, and told me a very curious story, which I can only recollect very vaguely, it was so peculiar. What I can recall is, that she was sent to gather wings. As soon as she had gathered a pair of wings for herself, she was to fly away, she said, to the country she came from; but where that was, she could give no information.

"She said she had to beg her wings from the butterflies and moths; and wherever she begged, no one refused her. But she needed a great many of the wings of butterflies and moths to make a pair for her; and so she had to wander about day after day, looking for butterflies, and night after night, looking for moths; and then she begged for their wings. But the day before, she had come into a part of the forest, she said, where there were multitudes of splendid butterflies flitting about, with wings which were just fit to make the eyes in the shoulders of hers; and she knew she could have as many of them as she liked for the asking; but as soon as she began to beg, there came a great creature right up to her, and threw her down, and walked over her. When she got up, she saw the wood was full of these beings stalking about, and seeming to have nothing to do with each other. As soon as ever she began to beg, one of them walked over her; till at last in dismay, and in growing horror of the senseless creatures, she had run away to look for somebody to help her. I asked her what they were like. She said, like great men, made of wood, without knee-or elbow-joints, and without any noses or mouths or eyes in their faces. I laughed at the little maiden, thinking she was making child's game of me; but, although she burst out laughing too, she persisted in asserting the truth of her story."

"'Only come, knight, come and see; I will lead you.'

"So I armed myself, to be ready for anything that might happen, and followed the child; for, though I could make nothing of her story, I could see she was a little human being in need of some help or other. As she walked before me, I looked attentively at her. Whether or not it was from being so often knocked down and walked over, I could not tell, but her clothes were very much torn, and in several places her white skin was peeping through. I thought she was hump-backed; but on looking more closely, I saw, through the tatters of her frock—do not laugh at me—a bunch on each shoulder, of the most gorgeous colours. Looking yet more closely, I saw that they were of the shape of folded wings, and were made of all kinds of butterfly-wings and moth-wings, crowded together like the feathers on the individual butterfly pinion; but, like them, most beautifully arranged, and producing a perfect harmony of colour and shade. I could now more easily believe the rest of her story; especially as I saw, every now and then, a certain heaving motion in the wings, as if they longed to be uplifted and outspread. But beneath her scanty garments complete wings could not be concealed, and indeed, from her own story, they were yet unfinished.

"After walking for two or three hours (how the little girl found her way, I could not imagine), we came to a part of the forest, the very air of which was quivering with the motions of multitudes of resplendent butterflies; as gorgeous in colour, as if the eyes of peacocks' feathers had taken to flight, but of infinite variety of hue and form, only that the appearance of some kind of eye on each wing predominated. 'There they are, there they are!' cried the child, in a tone of victory mingled with terror. Except for this tone, I should have thought she referred to the butterflies, for I could see nothing else. But at that moment an enormous butterfly, whose wings had great eyes of blue surrounded by confused cloudy heaps of more dingy colouring, just like a break in the clouds on a stormy day towards evening, settled near us. The child instantly began murmuring: 'Butterfly, butterfly, give me your wings'; when, the moment after, she fell to the ground, and began crying as if hurt. I drew my sword and heaved a great blow in the direction in which the child had fallen. It struck something, and instantly the most grotesque imitation of a man became visible. You see this Fairy Land is full of oddities and all sorts of incredibly ridiculous things, which a man is compelled to meet and treat as real existences, although all the time he feels foolish for doing so. This being, if being it could be called, was like a block of wood roughly hewn into the mere outlines of a man; and hardly so, for it had but head, body, legs, and arms—the head without a face, and the limbs utterly formless. I had hewn off one of its legs, but the two portions moved on as best they could, quite independent of each other; so that I had done no good. I ran after it, and clove it in twain from the head downwards; but it could not be convinced that its vocation was not to walk over people; for, as soon as the little girl began her begging again, all three parts came bustling up; and if I had not interposed my weight between her and them, she would have been trampled again under them. I saw that something else must be done. If the wood was full of the creatures, it would be an endless work to chop them so small that they could do no injury; and then, besides, the parts would be so numerous, that the butterflies would be in danger from the drift of flying chips. I served this one so, however; and then told the girl to beg again, and point out the direction in which one was coming. I was glad to find, however, that I could now see him myself, and wondered how they could have been invisible before. I would not allow him to walk over the child; but while I kept him off, and she began begging again, another appeared; and it was all I could do, from the weight of my armour, to protect her from the stupid, persevering efforts of the two. But suddenly the right plan occurred to me. I tripped one of them up, and, taking him by the legs, set him up on his head, with his heels against a tree. I was delighted to find he could not move. Meantime the poor child was walked over by the other, but it was for the last time. Whenever one appeared, I followed the same plan—tripped him up and set him on his head; and so the little beggar was able to gather her wings without any trouble, which occupation she continued for several hours in my company."

"What became of her?" I asked.

"I took her home with me to my castle, and she told me all her story; but it seemed to me, all the time, as if I were hearing a child talk in its sleep. I could not arrange her story in my mind at all, although it seemed to leave hers in some certain order of its own. My wife——"

Here the knight checked himself, and said no more. Neither did I urge the conversation farther.

Thus we journeyed for several days, resting at night in such shelter as we could get; and when no better was to be had, lying in the forest under some tree, on a couch of old leaves.

I loved the knight more and more. I believe never squire served his master with more care and joyfulness than I. I tended his horse; I cleaned his armour; my skill in the craft enabled me to repair it when necessary; I watched his needs; and was well repaid for all by the love itself which I bore him.

"This," I said to myself, "is a true man. I will serve him, and give him all worship, seeing in him the imbodiment of what I would fain become. If I cannot be noble myself, I will yet be servant to his nobleness." He, in return, soon showed me such signs of friendship and respect, as made my heart glad; and I felt that, after all, mine would be no lost life, if I might wait on him to the world's end, although no smile but his should greet me, and no one but him should say, "Well done! he was a good servant!" at last. But I burned to do something more for him than the ordinary routine of a squire's duty permitted.

One afternoon, we began to observe an appearance of roads in the wood. Branches had been cut down, and openings made, where footsteps had worn no path below. These indications increased as we passed on, till, at length, we came into a long, narrow avenue, formed by felling the trees in its line, as the remaining roots evidenced. At some little distance, on both hands, we observed signs of similar avenues, which appeared to converge with ours, towards one spot. Along these we indistinctly saw several forms moving, which seemed, with ourselves, to approach the common centre. Our path brought us, at last, up to a wall of yew-trees, growing close together, and intertwining their branches so, that nothing could be seen beyond it. An opening was cut in it like a door, and all the wall was trimmed smooth and perpendicular. The knight dismounted, and waited till I had provided for his horse's comfort; upon which we entered the place together.

It was a great space, bare of trees, and enclosed by four walls of yew, similar to that through which we had entered. These trees grew to a very great height, and did not divide from each other till close to the top, where their summits formed a row of conical battlements all around the walls. The space contained was a parallelogram of great length. Along each of the two longer sides of the interior, were ranged three ranks of men, in white robes, standing silent and solemn, each with a sword by his side, although the rest of his costume and bearing was more priestly than soldierly. For some distance inwards, the space between these opposite rows was filled with a company of men and women and children, in holiday attire. The looks of all were directed inwards, towards the further end. Far beyond the crowd, in a long avenue, seeming to narrow in the distance, went the long rows of the white-robed men. On what the attention of the multitude was fixed, we could not tell, for the sun had set before we arrived, and it was growing dark within. It grew darker and darker. The multitude waited in silence. The stars began to shine down into the enclosure, and they grew brighter and larger every moment. A wind arose, and swayed the pinnacles of the tree-tops; and made a strange sound, half like music, half like moaning, through the close branches and leaves of the tree-walls. A young girl who stood beside me, clothed in the same dress as the priests, bowed her head, and grew pale with awe.

The knight whispered to me, "How solemn it is! Surely they wait to hear the voice of a prophet. There is something good near!"

But I, though somewhat shaken by the feeling expressed by my master, yet had an unaccountable conviction that here was something bad. So I resolved to be keenly on the watch for what should follow.

Suddenly a great star, like a sun, appeared high in the air over the temple, illuminating it throughout; and a great song arose from the men in white, which went rolling round and round the building, now receding to the end, and now approaching, down the other side, the place where we stood. For some of the singers were regularly ceasing, and the next to them as regularly taking up the song, so that it crept onwards with gradations produced by changes which could not themselves be detected, for only a few of those who were singing ceased at the same moment. The song paused; and I saw a company of six of the white-robed men walk up the centre of the human avenue, surrounding a youth gorgeously attired beneath his robe of white, and wearing a chaplet of flowers on his head. I followed them closely, with my keenest observation; and, by accompanying their slow progress with my eyes, I was able to perceive more clearly what took place when they arrived at the other end. I knew that my sight was so much more keen than that of most people, that I had good reason to suppose I should see more than the rest could, at such a distance. At the farther end a throne stood upon a platform, high above the heads of the surrounding priests. To this platform I saw the company begin to ascend, apparently by an inclined plane or gentle slope. The throne itself was elevated again, on a kind of square pedestal, to the top of which led a flight of steps. On the throne sat a majestic-looking figure, whose posture seemed to indicate a mixture of pride and benignity, as he looked down on the multitude below. The company ascended to the foot of the throne, where they all kneeled for some minutes; then they rose and passed round to the side of the pedestal upon which the throne stood. Here they crowded close behind the youth, putting him in the foremost place, and one of them opened a door in the pedestal, for the youth to enter. I was sure I saw him shrink back, and those crowding behind pushed him in. Then, again, arose a burst of song from the multitude in white, which lasted some time. When it ceased, a new company of seven commenced its march up the centre. As they advanced, I looked up at my master: his noble countenance was full of reverence and awe. Incapable of evil himself, he could scarcely suspect it in another, much less in a multitude such as this, and surrounded with such appearances of solemnity. I was certain it was the really grand accompaniments that overcame him; that the stars overhead, the dark towering tops of the yew-trees, and the wind that, like an unseen spirit, sighed through their branches, bowed his spirit to the belief, that in all these ceremonies lay some great mystical meaning which, his humility told him, his ignorance prevented him from understanding.

More convinced than before, that there was evil here, I could not endure that my master should be deceived; that one like him, so pure and noble, should respect what, if my suspicions were true, was worse than the ordinary deceptions of priestcraft. I could not tell how far he might be led to countenance, and otherwise support their doings, before he should find cause to repent bitterly of his error. I watched the new procession yet more keenly, if possible, than the former. This time, the central figure was a girl; and, at the close, I observed, yet more indubitably, the shrinking back, and the crowding push. What happened to the victims, I never learned; but I had learned enough, and I could bear it no longer. I stooped, and whispered to the young girl who stood by me, to lend me her white garment. I wanted it, that I might not be entirely out of keeping with the solemnity, but might have at least this help to passing unquestioned. She looked up, half-amused and half-bewildered, as if doubting whether I was in earnest or not. But in her perplexity, she permitted me to unfasten it, and slip it down from her shoulders.

I easily got possession of it; and, sinking down on my knees in the crowd, I rose apparently in the habit of one of the worshippers.

Giving my battle-axe to the girl, to hold in pledge for the return of her stole, for I wished to test the matter unarmed, and, if it was a man that sat upon the throne, to attack him with hands bare, as I supposed his must be, I made my way through the crowd to the front, while the singing yet continued, desirous of reaching the platform while it was unoccupied by any of the priests. I was permitted to walk up the long avenue of white robes unmolested, though I saw questioning looks in many of the faces as I passed. I presume my coolness aided my passage; for I felt quite indifferent as to my own fate; not feeling, after the late events of my history, that I was at all worth taking care of; and enjoying, perhaps, something of an evil satisfaction, in the revenge I was thus taking upon the self which had fooled me so long. When I arrived on the platform, the song had just ceased, and I felt as if all were looking towards me. But instead of kneeling at its foot, I walked right up the stairs to the throne, laid hold of a great wooden image that seemed to sit upon it, and tried to hurl it from its seat. In this I failed at first, for I found it firmly fixed. But in dread lest, the first shock of amazement passing away, the guards would rush upon me before I had effected my purpose, I strained with all my might; and, with a noise as of the cracking, and breaking, and tearing of rotten wood, something gave way, and I hurled the image down the steps. Its displacement revealed a great hole in the throne, like the hollow of a decayed tree, going down apparently a great way. But I had no time to examine it, for, as I looked into it, up out of it rushed a great brute, like a wolf, but twice the size, and tumbled me headlong with itself, down the steps of the throne. As we fell, however, I caught it by the throat, and the moment we reached the platform, a struggle commenced, in which I soon got uppermost, with my hand upon its throat, and knee upon its heart. But now arose a wild cry of wrath and revenge and rescue. A universal hiss of steel, as every sword was swept from its scabbard, seemed to tear the very air in shreds. I heard the rush of hundreds towards the platform on which I knelt. I only tightened my grasp of the brute's throat. His eyes were already starting from his head, and his tongue was hanging out. My anxious hope was, that, even after they had killed me, they would be unable to undo my gripe of his throat, before the monster was past breathing. I therefore threw all my will, and force, and purpose, into the grasping hand. I remember no blow. A faintness came over me, and my consciousness departed.

CHAPTER XXIV

"We are ne'er like angels till our passions die."
DEKKER.

"This wretched Inn, where we scarce stay to bait,
We call our Dwelling-Place:
We call one Step a Race:
But angels in their full enlightened state,
Angels, who Live, and know what 'tis to Be,
Who all the nonsense of our language see,
Who speak things, and our words, their ill-drawn
pictures, scorn,
When we, by a foolish figure, say,
Behold an old man dead! then they
Speak properly, and cry, Behold a man-child born!"
COWLEY.

I was dead, and right content. I lay in my coffin, with my hands folded in peace. The knight, and the lady I loved, wept over me.
Her tears fell on my face.
"Ah!" said the knight, "I rushed amongst them like a madman. I hewed them down like brushwood. Their swords battered on me like hail, but hurt me not. I cut a lane through to my friend. He was dead. But he had throttled the monster, and I had to cut the handful out of its throat, before I could disengage and carry off his body. They dared not molest me as I brought him back."
"He has died well," said the lady.
My spirit rejoiced. They left me to my repose. I felt as if a cool hand had been laid upon my heart, and had stilled it. My soul was like a summer evening, after a heavy fall of rain, when the drops are yet glistening on the trees in the last rays of the down-going sun, and the wind of the twilight has begun to blow. The hot fever of life had gone by, and I breathed the clear mountain-air of the land of Death. I had never dreamed of such blessedness. It was not that I had in any way ceased to be what I had been. The very fact that anything can die, implies the

existence of something that cannot die; which must either take to itself another form, as when the seed that is sown dies, and arises again; or, in conscious existence, may, perhaps, continue to lead a purely spiritual life. If my passions were dead, the souls of the passions, those essential mysteries of the spirit which had imbodied themselves in the passions, and had given to them all their glory and wonderment, yet lived, yet glowed, with a pure, undying fire. They rose above their vanishing earthly garments, and disclosed themselves angels of light. But oh, how beautiful beyond the old form! I lay thus for a time, and lived as it were an unradiating existence; my soul a motionless lake, that received all things and gave nothing back; satisfied in still contemplation, and spiritual consciousness.

Ere long, they bore me to my grave. Never tired child lay down in his white bed, and heard the sound of his playthings being laid aside for the night, with a more luxurious satisfaction of repose than I knew, when I felt the coffin settle on the firm earth, and heard the sound of the falling mould upon its lid. It has not the same hollow rattle within the coffin, that it sends up to the edge of the grave. They buried me in no graveyard. They loved me too much for that, I thank them; but they laid me in the grounds of their own castle, amid many trees; where, as it was spring-time, were growing primroses, and blue-bells, and all the families of the woods

Now that I lay in her bosom, the whole earth, and each of her many births, was as a body to me, at my will. I seemed to feel the great heart of the mother beating into mine, and feeding me with her own life, her own essential being and nature. I heard the footsteps of my friends above, and they sent a thrill through my heart. I knew that the helpers had gone, and that the knight and the lady remained, and spoke low, gentle, tearful words of him who lay beneath the yet wounded sod. I rose into a single large primrose that grew by the edge of the grave, and from the window of its humble, trusting face, looked full in the countenance of the lady. I felt that I could manifest myself in the primrose; that it said a part of what I wanted to say; just as in the old time, I had used to betake myself to a song for the same end. The flower caught her eye. She stooped and plucked it, saying, "Oh, you beautiful creature!" and, lightly kissing it, put it in her bosom. It was the first kiss she had ever given me. But the flower soon began to wither, and I forsook it.

It was evening. The sun was below the horizon; but his rosy beams yet illuminated a feathery cloud, that floated high above the world. I arose, I reached the cloud; and, throwing myself upon it, floated with it in sight of the sinking sun. He sank, and the cloud grew gray; but the grayness touched not my heart. It carried its rose-hue within; for now I could love

147

without needing to be loved again. The moon came gliding up with all the past in her wan face. She changed my couch into a ghostly pallor, and threw all the earth below as to the bottom of a pale sea of dreams. But she could not make me sad. I knew now, that it is by loving, and not by being loved, that one can come nearest the soul of another; yea, that, where two love, it is the loving of each other, and not the being loved by each other, that originates and perfects and assures their blessedness. I knew that love gives to him that loveth, power over any soul beloved, even if that soul know him not, bringing him inwardly close to that spirit; a power that cannot be but for good; for in proportion as selfishness intrudes, the love ceases, and the power which springs therefrom dies. Yet all love will, one day, meet with its return. All true love will, one day, behold its own image in the eyes of the beloved, and be humbly glad. This is possible in the realms of lofty Death. "Ah! my friends," thought I, "how I will tend you, and wait upon you, and haunt you with my love."

"My floating chariot bore me over a great city. Its faint dull sound steamed up into the air—a sound—how composed?" How many hopeless cries," thought I, "and how many mad shouts go to make up the tumult, here so faint where I float in eternal peace, knowing that they will one day be stilled in the surrounding calm, and that despair dies into infinite hope, and the seeming impossible there, is the law here!

"But, O pale-faced women, and gloomy-browed men, and forgotten children, how I will wait on you, and minister to you, and, putting my arms about you in the dark, think hope into your hearts, when you fancy no one is near! Soon as my senses have all come back, and have grown accustomed to this new blessed life, I will be among you with the love that healeth."

With this, a pang and a terrible shudder went through me; a writhing as of death convulsed me; and I became once again conscious of a more limited, even a bodily and earthly life.

CHAPTER XXV

"Our life is no dream; but it ought to become one, and perhaps will."—NOVALIS.

"And on the ground, which is my modres gate,
I knocke with my staf, erlich and late,
And say to hire, Leve mother, let me in."

Sinking from such a state of ideal bliss, into the world of shadows which again closed around and infolded me, my first dread was, not unnaturally, that my own shadow had found me again, and that my torture had commenced anew. It was a sad revulsion of feeling. This, indeed, seemed to correspond to what we think death is, before we die. Yet I felt within me a power of calm endurance to which I had hitherto been a stranger. For, in truth, that I should be able if only to think such things as I had been thinking, was an unspeakable delight. An hour of such peace made the turmoil of a lifetime worth striving through.

I found myself lying in the open air, in the early morning, before sunrise. Over me rose the summer heaven, expectant of the sun. The clouds already saw him, coming from afar; and soon every dewdrop would rejoice in his individual presence within it.

I lay motionless for a few minutes; and then slowly rose and looked about me. I was on the summit of a little hill; a valley lay beneath, and a range of mountains closed up the view upon that side. But, to my horror, across the valley, and up the height of the opposing mountains, stretched, from my very feet, a hugely expanding shade. There it lay, long and large, dark and mighty. I turned away with a sick despair; when lo! I beheld the sun just lifting his head above the eastern hill, and the shadow that fell from me, lay only where his beams fell not. I danced for joy. It was only the natural shadow, that goes with every man who walks in the sun. As he arose, higher and higher, the shadow-head sank down the side of the opposite hill, and crept in across the valley towards my feet.

Now that I was so joyously delivered from this fear, I saw and recognised the country around me. In the valley below, lay my own castle, and the haunts of my childhood were all about me hastened home. My sisters received me with unspeakable joy; but I suppose they observed some change in me, for a kind of respect, with a slight touch of awe in it, mingled with their joy, and made me ashamed. They had been in great distress about me. On the morning of my disappearance, they had found the floor of my room flooded; and, all that day, a wondrous and nearly impervious mist had hung about the castle and grounds. I had been gone, they told me, twenty-one days. To me it seemed twenty-one years. Nor could I yet feel quite secure in my new experiences. When, at night, I lay down once more in my own bed, I did not feel at all sure that when I awoke, I should not find myself in some mysterious region of Fairy Land. My dreams were incessant and perturbed; but when I did awake, I saw clearly that I was in my own home.

My mind soon grew calm; and I began the duties of my new position, somewhat instructed, I hoped, by the adventures that had befallen me in Fairy Land. Could I translate the experience of my travels there, into common life? This was the question. Or must I live it all over again, and learn it all over again, in the other forms that belong to the world of men, whose experience yet runs parallel to that of Fairy Land? These questions I cannot answer yet. But I fear.

Even yet, I find myself looking round sometimes with anxiety, to see whether my shadow falls right away from the sun or no. I have never yet discovered any inclination to either side. And if I am not unfrequently sad, I yet cast no more of a shade on the earth, than most men who have lived in it as long as I. I have a strange feeling sometimes, that I am a ghost, sent into the world to minister to my fellow men, or, rather, to repair the wrongs I have already done.

May the world be brighter for me, at least in those portions of it, where my darkness falls not.

Thus I, who set out to find my Ideal, came back rejoicing that I had lost my Shadow.

When the thought of the blessedness I experienced, after my death in Fairy Land, is too high for me to lay hold upon it and hope in it, I often think of the wise woman in the cottage, and of her solemn assurance that she knew something too good to be told. When I am oppressed by any sorrow or real perplexity, I often feel as if I had only left her cottage for a time, and would soon return out of the vision, into it again. Sometimes, on such occasions, I find myself, unconsciously almost, looking about for the mystic mark of red, with the vague hope of entering her door, and being comforted by her wise tenderness. I then console myself by saying: "I have come through the door of Dismay; and the way back from the world into which that has led me, is through my tomb. Upon that the red sign lies, and I shall find it one day, and be glad."

I will end my story with the relation of an incident which befell me a few days ago. I had been with my reapers, and, when they ceased their work at noon, I had lain down under the shadow of a great, ancient beech-tree, that stood on the edge of the field. As I lay, with my eyes closed, I began to listen to the sound of the leaves overhead. At first, they made sweet inarticulate music alone; but, by-and-by, the sound seemed to begin to take shape, and to be gradually moulding itself into words; till, at last, I seemed able to distinguish these, half-dissolved in a little ocean of circumfluent tones: "A great good is coming—is coming—is coming to thee, Anodos;" and so over and over again. I fancied that the sound reminded me of the voice of the ancient woman, in the cottage that was four-square. I opened my eyes, and, for a moment, almost believed that I saw her face, with its many wrinkles and its young eyes, looking at me from between two hoary branches of the beech overhead. But when I looked more keenly, I saw only twigs and leaves, and the infinite sky, in tiny spots, gazing through between. Yet I know that good is coming to me—that good is always coming; though few have at all times the simplicity and the courage to believe it. What we call evil, is the only and best shape, which, for the person and his condition at the time, could be assumed by the best good. And so, *Farewell.*

Freeriver is a community project working to create a place for people to visit and potentially live, long-term, in peace, free from the normal stresses of modern life.

We aim to provide a place where people can spend time discovering themselves and discovering nature. We aim to focus on creativity, health and wellbeing. We plan to provide events and classes for people in the local area and enhance the community.

Please visit our website for more details

www.freerivercommunity.com
freerivercommunity@hotmail.com

www.freerivercommunity.com

Greville MacDonald (1856 in Bolton – 1944

George MacDonald (10 December 1824 – 18 September 1905)

Any profits generated from the sale of this book will go towards the Freeriver Community project, a project designed to promote harmonious community living and well-being in the world. To learn more about the Freeriver project please visit the website - www.freerivercommunity.com

Made in the USA
Monee, IL
08 April 2022